T0019792

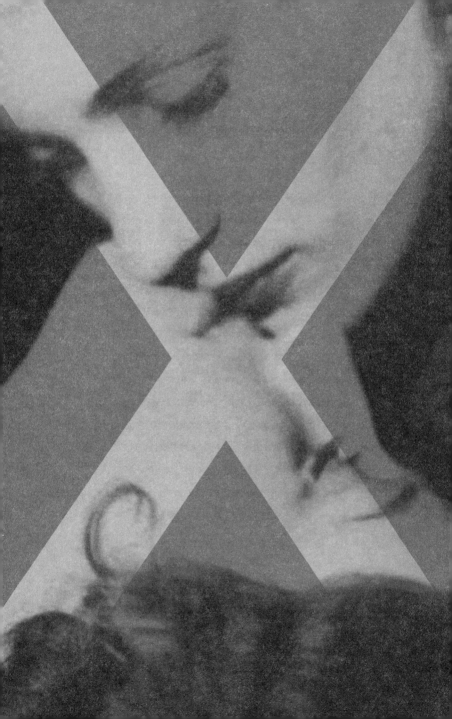

THÉRÈSE
AND
ISABELLE

VIOLETTE LEDUC

Translated by Sophie Lewis
Afterwords by
Michael Lucey and Carlo Jansiti

THE FEMINIST PRESS
AT THE CITY UNIVERSITY OF NEW YORK
NEW YORK CITY

Published in 2015 by the Feminist Press
at the City University of New York
The Graduate Center
365 Fifth Avenue, Suite 5406
New York, NY 10016
feministpress.org

First Feminist Press edition 2015

Second printing July 2020

Cover design by Herb Thornby, herbthornby.com
Text design by Drew Stevens

Library of Congress Cataloging-in-Publication Data

Leduc, Violette, 1907-1972.
[Thérèse et Isabelle. English]
Therese and Isabelle / Violette Leduc. — First Feminist Press edition.
    pages cm
Published in French as Thérèse et Isabelle (Éditions Gallimard, Paris,
1966 and 2000).
"Translation copyright © 2012 by Sophie Lewis" — Verso title page.
    ISBN 978-1-55861-889-3 (pbk.) ISBN 978-1-55861-894-7 (ebook)
1. Lesbians—Fiction. 2. France—Fiction. I. Lewis, Sophie, translator.
II. Title.
PQ2623.E3657T513 2015
843'.914—dc23

                                                              2014042675

CONTENTS

THÉRÈSE
AND
ISABELLE

We began the week every Sunday evening in the shoe room. We polished our shoes, which had been brushed at home that morning in our kitchens or gardens. We came in from the town; we were not hungry. Keeping away from the refectory until Monday morning, we would make a few rounds of the schoolyard, then go two by two into the shoe room accompanied by our bored supervisor. The shoe room at our school was nothing like those street stands where all the nailing, the shaping, the hammering send your feet hurrying back to the pavement outside. We polished in a poorly lit, windowless chapel of monotony; we daydreamed with our shoes on our knees, those evenings that we came back to school. The virtuous scent of polish that revives us in pharmacies here made us melancholy. We were languishing over our cloths, we were awkward, our grace had abandoned us. The new monitor sat with us on the bench, reading aloud and lost in her tale, gazing far beyond the town, beyond the school, while we carried on stroking leather with wool in the half-light. That evening we were ten pallid returnees in the waiting-room gloom, ten returnees who said not a word to each other, ten sullen girls all alike and avoiding each other.

My future will be nothing like theirs. I have no future at the school. My mother said so. If I miss you too much I'll take you home again. School is not a boat for the other boarders. She might take me back home at any moment. I am only temporarily on board. She could take me out of school on a first day of term, she could take me back this evening. Thirty days. Thirty days I've been a passenger at the school. I want to live here, I want to polish my shoes in the shoe room. Marthe will not be called back home . . . Julienne will not be called home . . . Isabelle will not be called home . . . They are certain of their futures, although I'm willing to bet that Isabelle spits on the school each time she spits on her shoe. My polish would be softer if I spat as she does. I could spread it further. She is lucky. Her parents are teachers. Who is going to snatch her away from school? She spits. Perhaps she is angry, the school's best student . . . I am spitting like her, I moisten my polish but where will I be a month from now? I am the bad student, the worst student in the big dormitory. I don't care in the least. I detest the head-mistress, spit my girl, spit on your polish, I hate sewing, gymnastics, chemistry, I hate everything and I avoid my companions. It's sad but I don't want to leave this place. My mother has married someone, my mother has betrayed me.

The brush has fallen from my knees, Isabelle has kicked my polish brush away while I was thinking.

"My brush, my brush!"

Isabelle lowers her head, she spits harder on the box calf. The brush rolls up to the monitor's foot. You'll pay for that kick of yours. I collect the object, I wrench Isabelle's face around, I dig my fingers in, I stuff the rag blotched with wax, dust, and red polish into her eyes, into her mouth; I look at her milky skin inside the collar of her uniform, I lift my hand from her face, I return to my place. Silent and furious, Isabelle cleans her eyes and lips, she spits a sixth time on the shoe, she hunches her shoulders, the monitor closes her book, claps her hands, the light flickers. Isabelle goes back to shining her shoe.

We were waiting for her. She had her legs crossed, rubbing hard. "You must come now," said the new monitor timidly. We had come into the shoe room with clattering heels but we left muted by our black slippers like phoney orphans. Close cousins to the espadrille, our slippers, our Silent Sisters, stifle wherever they step: stone; wood; earth. Angels would lend us their heels as we left the shoe room with cozy melancholy flowing from our souls down into our slippers. Every Sunday we went up to the dormitory with the monitor; all the way there we would breathe in the rose-scented disinfectant. Isabelle had caught up with us on the stairs. I hate her, I want to hate her. I would feel better if I hated her more. Tomorrow I'll have her at my table in the refectory again. She's in charge of it. She's in charge of the table I eat at in the refectory. I cannot change my table. Her sidelong little smile when I sit down late. I've put that sly little smile straight. That natural insouciance . . . I'll straighten out that natural insouciance of hers too. I'll go to the headmistress if necessary but I shall change my table in the refectory.

We entered a dormitory in which the dim sheen of the linoleum foretold the solitude of walking there at midnight. We drew aside our percale curtains and found ourselves in our unlockable, wall-less bedrooms. Isabelle's curtain rings shunted along their rail just after the others'. The night monitor paced along the passage. We opened our cases, took out our underwear, folded it away on the shelves in our wardrobes, keeping out the sheets for our narrow beds, we threw the key into the case which we now closed for the week, we put that away in the wardrobe too, and made our beds. Under the institutional lighting our things were no longer ours. We stepped out of our uniforms, hung them up ready for Thursday's walk, folded our underpants, laid them on the chair, and took out our nightgowns.

Isabelle left the dormitory with her pitcher.

I listen to the tassel of her gown rustling over the linoleum. I hear her fingers' drumming on the enamel. Her box opposite mine. That's what I have in front of me. Her coming and going. I watch for them, her comings and goings. Were you tight? Got good and tight? This is what she says when I come in late to the refectory. I'll flatten that sarcastic smile of hers. I didn't get tight. I was practicing diminished minor arpeggios. She is scornful because I hide away in the music room. She says that I make a din, that she can hear me from the prep room. It is true: I do practice but all I make is noise. Her again, always her, again her on the stairs. I run into her. I would have undressed slowly if I had known she was at the tap fetching water. Shall I run away? Come back later when she is gone? I won't go. I am not afraid of her: I hate her. She has her back to me. What nonchalance . . . She knows there is someone right behind her but she will not hurry. I would say she was provoking me if she knew that it was I but she doesn't know. She is not curious enough even to check who is behind her. I would not have come if I'd known she would be dawdling here. I thought she was far away—she is right here. Soon her pitcher will be full. At last. I know that long, loose hair of hers, there's nothing new about her hair for she walks about like that in the passage. Excuse me. She said excuse me. She brushed my face with her hair while I was thinking about it. It is beyond belief. She has tossed her hair back so as to send it into my face. Her mass of hair was on my lips. She didn't know I was behind her and she flicked her hair in my face! She didn't know I was behind her and she has said excuse me. It is unbelievable. She would not say I'm keeping you, I'm being slow, the tap isn't working. She tosses her hair at you while asking you to excuse her. The water flows more slowly. She has touched the tap. I will not speak to her, the water has almost stopped, you will not prize a word out of me. You ignore me, I shall ignore you. Why did you want me to wait? Is that what you wanted? I shall not speak to you. If you have time to spare, I have time too.

The monitor has called us from out in the passage, as if we were in league together. Isabelle went out to her.

I heard her lying, explaining to the new monitor that the tap had gone dry.

The monitor is talking to her through the percale curtain: are you eighteen? We are almost the same age, says the monitor. Their conversation is cut short by the whistle of a train escaping from the station that we left at seven. Isabelle soaps her skin. Tight . . . Did you get good and tight? Who can say what she is thinking? This is a girl with something on her mind. She's dreaming or else she spits; she dreams and works harder than the rest.

"And you, how old are you?" the new monitor asked me.

Isabelle will find out my age. "Seventeen," I mutter. "Are you in the same class?" asks the monitor. "Yes, in the same class," replies Isabelle, energetically rinsing out her wash glove. "She's lying to you," I shout. "You don't see she's making fun of you. I am not in her class and I don't care."

"Remember your manners," says the monitor to me.

I opened my curtain a crack: the supervisor was moving away, returning to his reading in the passage, Isabelle was giggling in her box, another girl was up to something with her sweet wrappers.

"I have strict orders," whispered the new monitor. "No visitors in the boxes. Each girl in her own."

We were always under threat of an evening inspection by the headmistress. We would tidy our comb, our nailbrush, our washbowl, and lie down in our anonymous beds as if on a small medical ward. As soon as we had finished washing and tidying, we would present ourselves for the monitor's inspection, neat and tidy and in bed. Some students offered her pastries, detained her with flattering sweet talk, while Isabelle withdrew into her tomb. As soon as I had recreated my nest in the cold bed, I forgot about Isabelle, but if I woke, I thought of her again, to hate her. She did not dream aloud, her bedstead did not creak. One night, at two o'clock, I got up, crossed the passage, held my breath, and listened to her sleeping. She was not there. She even mocked me in her sleep. I had gripped her curtain. I had stayed there listening. She was gone; she had the last word. I hated her between sleeping and waking: in the morning bell at half past six, in the low tone of her voice, in the splashing and draining sounds as she washed, her hand snapping closed the box of dental paste. All one can hear is her, I told myself stubbornly. I hated the dust from her room, when she let the duster poke under my curtain, when she tapped her fingers on our partitions, when she thrust her fist into her percale curtain. She spoke rarely, she made the movements required of her, in the dormitory, the refectory, in the rows of girls; she cut herself off, brooding in the schoolyard. I wondered what gave her cause for such aloofness. She was studious but without either self-importance or zeal. Often Isabelle would slip my tunic belt undone; she played cool if I grew angry. She would start the day with this childish tease and straight away retie the belt at my back, humiliating me twice over instead of once.

I got up, wary as a smuggler. The new monitor stopped cleaning her nails. I waited. Isabelle, who never coughed, coughed: tonight she had stayed awake. I blocked her out and plunged my arm up to the shoulder into the drab cloth bag hanging in my wardrobe. Hidden inside this bag of dirty laundry were some books and my flashlight. I used to read at night. That evening I got back into bed without any appetite for reading, with the book, with the flashlight. I turned on the flashlight, I gazed lovingly at my Silent Sisters under the chair. The artificial moonlight coming from the monitor's room sucked the color from the contents of my cell.

I turned out the light; a girl crumpled some paper, I pushed away my book with a disappointed hand. Deader than a corpse, I thought to myself, picturing Isabelle lying stiff as a poker in her nightgown. The book was closed, the flashlight buried in the bed-covers. I put my hands together and prayed wordlessly; I asked for a world unknown to me, I listened, near my stomach, to the haze inside the seashell. The monitor also turned her light out. That lucky girl is asleep, lucky thing, she has a tomb to be lost in. The lucid ticking of my watch on the bedside table made my decision for me. I took up my book again and read beneath the covers.

Someone was spying behind my curtain. Hidden under the cover, I could still hear the inexorable ticktock. A night train left the station, left it to follow the monstrous whistle that was piercing the school's alien shadows. I threw back the bedcover; I was afraid of the comatose dormitory.

Someone was calling from behind the percale curtain.

I played dead. I pulled the cover back over my head and relit the flashlight.

"Thérèse," someone called into my box.

I turned it off.

"What are you doing under your covers?" asked the voice, which I didn't recognize.

"I'm reading."

They tore off my sheet and pulled my hair.

"I told you I'm reading!"

"Quietly," said Isabelle.

Another girl coughed.

"You can tell on me if you like."

She will not tell on me. I am unfair to her and I know it is unfair to say that to her.

"You weren't asleep? I thought you were the best sleeper in the dormitory."

"Softer," she said.

I whispered too loudly, I wanted to be done with this joy: I was elated to the point of pride.

Visiting me, Isabelle came no further than my percale curtain. I was suspicious of her shyness, suspicious of her long, loose hair in my cell.

"I'm afraid you're going to say no. Say you'll say yes," gasped Isabelle.

I had lit my flashlight; in spite of myself I had some consideration for my visitor.

"Say yes!" whispered Isabelle.

She was pressing a finger down on my dressing table.

She gripped her gown cord, pulling the gown tight around her. Her hair tumbled down over her orchards, her face grew older.

"What are you reading?"

She lifted her finger off the dressing table.

"I was beginning it when you came in."

I turned out the light because she was looking at my book.

"The name . . . tell me the name of the book."

"*A Happy Man.*"

"That's a title? Is it good?"

"I don't know. I just began."

Isabelle turned on her heel; a curtain ring slid along the rail. I thought she might be disappearing back into her tomb. She stopped.

"Come and read in my room."

She was leaving again, creating a distance between her request and my reply.

"Will you come? Say yes?"

"I don't know."

She left my box.

I could not regain my breath or my routine. She went back to her bed, her refuge. I wanted her immobile, lying still while I left my bed, my refuge. Isabelle had seen me with the sheets up to my neck. She did not know that I was wearing a special nightgown, a nightgown all stitched in honeycomb panels. I used to believe that personality came from outside us, from clothes that were different from those of other people. My visitor had crumpled my nightclothes without touching them, without knowing of them. The silk muslin nightgown slipped around my hips with the softness of a cobweb. I put my boarder's tunic on; I left my box with my wrists held tight in the elasticated cuffs of my regulation smock. The monitor was sleeping. I paused before the percale curtain. I entered.

"What's the time?" I exclaimed brightly.

I stayed standing by the curtains, pointing my flashlight toward her night table.

"Come in, there is room . . ."

I could not get used to her long, loose hair, the hair of a stranger who intimidated me. Isabelle checked the time.

"Won't you come in?" she said to her watch.

The opulence of that hair, which swept over the bars at the head of her bed, over her shoulders, the night table, the lace mat, enveloped me. This sheer screen that glistened, that hid the face of a girl reclining in a hospital room, frightened me. I switched off the flashlight.

Isabelle got up. She took the book from me, and the flashlight.

"Come now," she said.

She had got back into bed.

From her bed, she shone the flashlight at me.

I came forward. Isabelle was gently patting her hair.

I sat down on the mattress edge. She reached over my shoulder, she picked up my book from the table, gave it to me, reassured me. I leafed through it since she was staring at me; I didn't know which page to stop at. She was waiting for whatever I was waiting for. I fixed on the capital letter of the first sentence.

"Eleven o'clock," Isabelle said.

We wanted to hear the impact and the dying away of the school clock's eleven strokes. I stared at words on the first page without seeing anything. She took back my book, turned off the light.

Isabelle pulled me backward, she laid me down across the eiderdown, lifted me, held me in her arms: she was releasing me from a world I had never lived in to launch me into one I could not yet inhabit. With her lips she parted mine, moistened my clenched teeth. The fleshiness of her tongue frightened me: the foreign sex did not enter. I waited, withdrawn, contemplative. The lips wandered over my lips: a dusting of petals. My heart was beating too loudly and I wanted to listen to this seal of sweetness, this soft new tracing. Isabelle is kissing me, I tell myself. She was drawing a circle around my mouth, she encircled my trouble, put a cool kiss at each corner, she dived down to place two notes, returned, rested. Beneath their lids my eyes were wide with astonishment, the thundering of the conch shells too vast. Isabelle continued: we descended knot by knot into a night beyond the school's night, beyond the night of the town and of the tram depot. She had made her honey on my lips, the sphinxes had gone to sleep once more. I realized that I had been missing her even before we met. She listened to all she gave me, she kissed condensation on a window.

Isabelle tossed away her hair under which we had sheltered.

"Do you think she's asleep?" Isabelle asked.

"The monitor?"

"She's asleep," Isabelle decided.

"She's asleep," I agreed.

"You're shivering. Take off your nightgown, come here."

She drew back the covers.

"Come without the light," Isabelle said.

She stretched out against the partition, in her bed, at ease. I took off my gown, I felt too new standing on the carpet of an ancient world. I had to rush to her straight away for the ground would not support me. I lay down on the edge of the mattress, ready to creep away like a thief.

"You are cold. Come closer," said Isabelle.

A sleeping girl coughed, tried to divide us.

Already she is holding me back, already I was being held back, already we tormented each other, but the joyful foot that was touching mine, the ankle rubbing against my ankle, reassured. My nightgown tickled me while we embraced and swayed together. We had stopped, we had returned to memories of the dormitory, we listened to the night. Isabelle turned on the light: she wanted to see my face. I took the light from her. Lifted by a great wave, Isabelle slipped into bed, rose, plunged her face to mine, hugged me tightly. The roses were fraying from the belt she put around me. I put the same belt around her. And yet I wavered. I did not dare.

"The bed mustn't squeak," she said.

I looked for a cool place in the pillow, as if it were there that the bed would not squeak; I found a pillow of blond hair. Isabelle gathered me to her.

We embraced again, we wanted to engulf each other. We had cast off our families, the world, time, certainty. Clasping her against my gaping open heart, I wanted to draw Isabelle inside. Love is an exhausting invention. Isabelle, Thérèse, I pronounced in my head, getting used to the magical simplicity of our two names.

She swaddled my shoulders in the ermine of her arm, placed my hand in the channel between her breasts, on the fabric of her nightgown. Enchantment of my hand beneath hers, of my neck, my shoulders clothed by her arm. Yet my face was alone, my eyelids growing cold. Isabelle knew it. Trying to warm me up all over, her tongue danced at my teeth. I closed up, barricaded myself inside my mouth. She waited: this is how she taught me to open myself, to blossom. She was my body's secret muse. Her tongue, her little flame, charmed my blood, my flesh. I responded, provoked, fought, tried to be more violent than she. The slap of lips, the hiss of saliva became nothing to us. We labored hard, but as we slowed once more, in unison, grew careful, the draught grew richer. After so much saliva passed between them, our lips parted in spite of us. Isabelle dropped into the hollow of my shoulder.

"A train," she said, so as to catch her breath.

Something is crawling in my belly. I am frightened: there is an octopus in my belly.

Isabelle drew a childish mouth shape on my lips with her finger. The finger dropped from my lips to my neck. I seized it, drew it along my eyelashes:

"They are yours," I told her.

Isabelle is silent. Isabelle does not move. If she's asleep, it's over. Isabelle has returned to her ways. I don't believe in her anymore. I have to go. Her box is no longer mine. I cannot get up. We have not finished. I don't know anything but I know we haven't finished. If she's asleep, it is abduction. Isabelle drives me away while she sleeps. Make her not sleep, make it so the night will not end our night. Isabelle is not asleep!

She lifted my arm, she nuzzled at my armpit. My hips were growing pale. I felt a cold pleasure. I was not used to receiving so much. I listened to what she took and what she gave, I shimmered with gratitude: I suckled her. Isabelle threw herself elsewhere. She smoothed my hair, she stroked the midnight in my hair and the midnight trickled down my cheeks. She stopped, marked an interval. Forehead to forehead, we listened to the swirl, we abandoned ourselves to the silence, gave ourselves to it.

A caress is to a shiver as dusk is to a lightning flash. Isabelle shone a rake of light from my shoulder all the way to my wrist, ran her five-fingered reflector along my neck, over my nape, behind me. I was following her hand, I saw through half-closed eyes a neck, a shoulder, an arm that were not my neck, my shoulder, my arm. She ravished my ear as she had ravished my mouth with her mouth. The move was cynical, the sensation singular. I froze, I was frightened by this refinement of animality. Isabelle took me again, held me still by the hair, began again. The icy fingering shocked me, Isabelle's serenity reassured.

She leant out of the bed and opened a drawer in her night table. I seized her hand:

"A lace! Why a shoelace?"

"I'm tying up my hair. Be quiet or you'll get us caught."

Isabelle was tightening the knot, preparing herself.

She whom I awaited had come prepared. I was listening to what is huge, what is alone: the heart. A small blueish egg fell from her lips where she had left me, where she took me up again. She opened the collar of my nightgown, confirmed my shoulder's curve with her forehead, with her cheek. I accepted the wonders she was imagining on the curve of my shoulder. She was giv-

ing me a lesson in humility. I took fright.
I am flesh and blood, I am alive. I am not
an idol.

"Not so much!" I begged.

She closed my collar.

"Am I too heavy for you?" she asked
gently.

"Don't leave . . ."

I wanted to clasp her in my arms but
I didn't dare. The clock spat out quarter
hour after quarter hour; Isabelle was tracing a snail with her finger in that poor little space we have beneath our earlobes. She
was tickling me in spite of herself. It was
bizarre.

"Harder," I begged.

She took my head in her hands as if I
had been beheaded, she drove her tongue
into my mouth. She wanted us wasted,
lacerating. We were tearing each other to
pieces with stone needles. The kiss slowed
in my guts, it vanished, a hot current in the
sea.

"Again."

"For ages."

We stopped kissing, lay down and, phalanx to phalanx, we charged our finger bones with what we didn't know to say to each other.

Isabelle coughed and our interlaced fingers went silent.

"Let yourself go," she said.

She kissed the points of my collar, the red braid on my nightgown, she molded the bounty of our shoulders. Her careful hand traced lines over my lines, curves upon my curves. I glimpsed the halo of my revived shoulder, I listened to the light in her caress.

I stopped her.

"Let me go on," said Isabelle.

Her voice lingered, her hand sank into the covers. I felt the shape of Isabelle's neck, shoulder, and arm along my neck, encircling my shoulder, the length of my arm.

A flower opened in every pore of my skin. I took her arm and thanked her with a purple kiss upon the veins.

"You are kind, you are good," I said.

"You say I am good!"

"What can I do for you?"

The poverty of my vocabulary discouraged me. Isabelle's hands were shaking, they were adjusting a muslin corselette over the fabric of my nightgown: her hands were shaking with a maniac fervor.

She sat up on the bed, seized my waist. Isabelle rubbed her cheek against mine, she told a comforting tale with her cheek. She dropped her hands to my chest. We listened to the meowing of a cat in the main courtyard.

Isabelle's fingers opened, closed again like daisy buds, they freed breasts from rose-shaded purgatory. I was waking into spring with the babbling of lilacs under my skin.

"Come, come here again," I said.

Isabelle stroked my hip. My skin caressed became a caress; stroked, my hip shone through my intoxicated limbs into my languid ankles. It was torture, tiny tortures, in my belly.

"I can't go on."

We waited, we kept a sharp lookout for the shadows.

I took her in my arms but I did not embrace her as I wanted in that narrow bed, I did not engrave her in me. A peremptory little girl appeared:

"I want, I want."

I want what she wants, if the creeping octopus would leave me, if stars would stop shooting down my limbs. I await a flood of stones.

"Come back, come back . . ."

"You aren't helping me," said Isabelle.

The hand advanced under the fabric. I listened to the hand's coolness; it listened to my skin's heat. The finger explored where the two cheeks touch. It entered the gap, came out again. Isabelle caressed the two cheeks at once with one hand. My knees, my feet were crumbling away.

"It's too much. I tell you it's too much."

Indifferent, Isabelle stroked quickly, on and on.

It was torment, it was hot prickling. Isabelle fell forward onto me.

"Are you happy?"

"Yes," I say, dissatisfied.

She slipped into bed, laid her cheek on my belly; she listened to her child, for it was there that my heart was beating. I held out my arm, reached her face, her mouth, her hair so far from mine, my body was calmly wretched:

"Come back. I'm alone."

". . ."

The weight of the head that slipped into my crotch was frightening.

She was coming back, she was offering me a kiss with her good girl's lips on mine.

Isabelle clawed at the fabric over my pubic hair, she entered, withdrew, while not entering and not withdrawing; she rocked me, her fingers, the fabric, the time.

"Are you happy?"

"Yes Isabelle."

My politeness annoyed me.

Isabelle persevered differently, one monotonous finger on a single lip. My body took on the light of that finger as sand takes up water.

"Later," she said, into my neck.

"You want me to go now? I must go back to my box?"

"You must."

"You want us to part?"

"Yes."

There was a storm somewhere near my heart:

"Look, it's too early."

"Think of this evening, think of our other evenings. You aren't tired but soon you will be," said Isabelle.

I stood up, focused my flashlight, I licked my lips but found none of the salt from Isabelle's lips.

We leaned together over her watch, avoided catching each other's gaze.

"Take care when you cross the passage."

"I shan't take care."

I left.

Here you are again, you abandoned things. My bed is no longer my bed. You will do my bidding, things, otherwise I shall crush you. I have a museum of relics in the box opposite mine. She said it's enough. Now is a night of obstacles. Her smell belongs to me. I have lost her smell. Give me back her smell. Is she sleeping? Yes, she is asleep inside the tomb that is her bed, she is savoring the oblivion of her pillow. She is sending me away: she has taken all of me. I cannot rest on what no longer exists. I hurl my flashlight away, I worry at the bars of my bed, I bite the soap, chew the dental paste, scratch myself, punish myself.

I turn on the light, turn it off, turn on, turn off. I signal even through her sleep that I'm awake, that I am waiting for her. I turn on, turn off, I want to shut off her breathing. I want to see her again.

I left my box, stopped there before her curtain, my hope fixed on the orange light between my fingers.

Her name, my devotion.

The other girls and the monitor stuff themselves with darkness and with absence. I stay watching, I scorn all that.

"Are you sleeping?" I whisper, wanting the reassurance.

Words extracted from the silence and delivered into shadows.

I go into her box, approach the cadaver.

Blind and deaf, Isabelle plots, looking upon a world with the eyes of sleep. The obsession with rest resides behind the sleeper's forehead. Like the last of the magi, I lean over her. I try but I dare not wake her. A sleeper never completes her work.

I turn out the light: the silence lies close on my temples. I turn it on: the sleeper is lying on her back, she makes an offering of her face to the ceiling, she poses on the pillow like a invalid suffering even in her sleep, she drags along her sleeper's inheritance which we shall never know. I sit down at the foot of the bed, on the soft eiderdown that slips off, I stare at her, I do not decipher. I touch my own hand—for that of the deeply breathing statue. She is sleeping without an eiderdown. She will get cold. So this is not merely a rock upon a platform. I go nearer. I steal the scent of hyacinths from her sleeping mouth, I lift her, hold her to me tightly until I'm seized by a mad happiness that makes me laugh. I laugh. Isabelle awakens at my lips. What a Christmas . . . I have waited so long for the opening of those lids, wished so much for my rebirth in her eyes.

"Didn't you go?"

"I came back."

She seems to be reflecting. No. She is resting, prolonging her cure of oblivion in my eyes. She speaks:

"Were you there watching me?"

"What? Say it quickly."

"Nothing. Tomorrow . . ."

"It is tomorrow. Say it, say it."

"Nothing."

She falls back on the pillow. Refreshed Isabelle abandons my arms, my hands. The nonchalante will go back to sleep.

"Don't disappear!"

My alarm distracts her.

"Come back to my mouth," she says.

At last she stirs, she says it into my hair, near my ear, and I turn out the light for the abyss inside a kiss.

"You sleep while I am here."

"Was I sleeping?"

"While you were sleeping we were separated."

Isabelle listens to me with all her soul.

"I was unhappy. You're not sleeping now?"

"You must forgive me. I was so sleepy. And you, you haven't slept?"

"No. I was waiting."

"I promise I will not sleep when you are here."

"Oh, you promise," I said.

I hid my face in my arms.

"Are you crying?"

"I'm not crying."

"If you cry we will be caught," says Isabelle.

"Then we'll be caught. So what?"

"Aren't you looking forward to tomorrow evening?"

"Let's run away. Tomorrow we will be free."

"Keep your voice down," she says.

"You don't want to. Why?"

"Because it's impossible."

"I'm going for good," I say.

I left once more.

Isabelle followed me into the passage:

"You think we'll be able to embrace when we've a policeman on either side!"

She pulled me back into her box, she encircled me anew while I pretended to resist her. It was the first time that she clasped me to her standing up.

We listened to the vortex of heavenly bodies deep within us, we watched the shadows whirling in the dormitory.

I brought Isabelle back from a chilly winter seafront, I drew back the sheets, showed her the way:

"It is late. Sleep. I was wrong just now: you must sleep."

"No!"

"You're yawning."

"Come closer. I want to see you."

The flashlight was hurting her eyes. Soon that slack mask would cover her face.

"Don't sleep . . ."

"I promise I won't."

I wait, I watch her. I wait: the spider spins deep inside me, the spider will pounce at my sex if I don't ask . . . What is there to ask?

She wonders how long I will last with her drug in my eyes. Our complicity shudders between us, sends waves, while my judge silently judges the future's kisses and caresses. I look at her as I look at the sea in the evening when I can no longer see it.

"It's time to go," says Isabelle.

We would rise at half past six. The monitors would push the curtain rings along their rails, coming into our cells to see that we were up. We would strip our beds, wash in cold water while our mattresses grew cold, remake our beds once we had dressed. At a quarter to seven, the girl on duty would open the cupboard, take out the dustpan and broom, clean her cell, leave the broom outside her neighbor's box. At twenty-five past seven, the monitor inspected our combs, at twenty-five past seven we made sure our hands and nails were impeccable, at twenty-five past seven the bell would ring: we lined up in the passage and went down the stairs two by two. At half past seven we put our shoes on in the shoe room, at seven thirty-five we broke out of our pairs in the hall and formed groups according to our own alliances. At seven forty the porter rang the bell once. The girls lined up in the hall. We would go as far as the refectory, take earthenware pitchers from their rack, butter symmetrical pieces of bread. At ten to eight the headmistress came in. We put down our buttered bread, we stood to attention. At eight o'clock the head monitor clapped her hands. We would rise from the tables, replace the pitchers, push our chairs in against the table, sweep our crumbs into our bowls, and line up two by two in the passage. Girls flew off toward their violins, their primers, their pianos. We took a few turns around the schoolyard, lined up once again to go up to the study room, took our books from our lockers, and studied until half past eight.

On Monday morning I made a solemn entrance into the refectory, with Isabelle on my right: we were progressing down the great aisle of a photographer's salon on our wedding day. I stepped around some bouquets of white flowers and sat down. In fact, she wasn't following me. My wedding ended in a billow of chattering, in the disquieting flavor of milky ersatz coffee sweetened with saccharin. I had been torn from her, my ribs ached. She ignored me in the passage, she lingered in bleached strips of sunlight as it filtered through the windows. I looked at the vase on the table, I wanted it as fortification.

"I wish you would look at me when I'm looking at you," she said behind me.

She lifted the bread basket, put it back in the same place; she walked off nonchalantly, her hands loosening the belt around her slim waist.

She buttered some pieces of bread, stuck the halves together, pulled them open, looked at them, she wasn't eating. She leaned on her elbows, she turned toward a girl who was talking to her.

I know the secret of that thick-coiled hair, I know those two great tortoiseshell hairpins lying on her nightstand. I am looking at you, I am looking at you, my eyes call out to her. The whip of her long, loose hair last night whips through my insides hazily. What am I guilty of? ask her coaxing eyes. I cannot tell her that from here her arms' aroma is lily of the valley; her twisted hair, of midday's loaves in the bakers' baskets; her cheek, of elder after the rain; my lips, of the Noirmoutiers marshes' salt; her throat, of the shadowy scent of black currants.

I glimpse that Isabelle has folded her napkin, tossed her bowl to the devil. I asked the girl if I might do her duty for her. I collected the dishes, I ate the crumbs left in Isabelle's bowl and, amidst the general indifference, I fed myself on the slops.

Her chair fell backward, Isabelle was hysterical at the table, the head monitor ran to her. Girls stood up, surrounded Isabelle. I had no right to approach her: I was no longer innocent.

The monitor was stroking her hair, she was whispering into her ear in front of the sheepish girls. I felt cast off. "What is the matter?" hummed the red-haired monitor. Two kneeling girls were stroking her hand, touching her breast, edging toward her heart.

She will die, for the whole school is pawing at her!

"Does lemon bleach your hands?" I ask my neighbor at the table.

I say things I'm not thinking. Don't let her die. She will not die. We two are immortals. What an affront, if she should die.

"Isabelle is ill," I say.

"Faking it," says the girl.

"Isabelle is ill. Shut up."

I'll cut their goody-goody hands from around her shoulders. I'll cut them off.

Isabelle lifted her head. She said:

"I don't know what was wrong with me."

The monitor, the girls dropped back. I went up to her:

"What was wrong with you?"

"Needing you."

The girls rose and reformed their lines. Isabelle touched her finger to my shoulder. The touch meant: I'll tell if you tell; I'll stumble if you stumble; I shall waste away if you waste away.

I stood beside her: my elbow fit perfectly into her palm. She gave the ghost of an embrace; the girls were dispersing. We were still walking in step; we wanted space and solemn distance to keep us apart. Yes, we wanted to be ceremonial in the playground. She drew away.

Images scattered around Isabelle as she drew away: the birdsong in our tree-less courtyard was a cool shaft marking the day's beginning, the song suggested clear-ings on the outskirts of towns; Isabelle was drawing away. I wanted to be stone, a stone with holes for eyes. I thought I would cure myself of her by looking at the sky; I fol-lowed the shifting of the monster stretched out across it: a fraying, the figure of a skier drawn on a blue ground with a pencil of snow. A figure I had not seen taking shape. The monster perished as I observed it, the bird fell silent, Isabelle disappeared; where the cloud had been, the recast sky looked like an oil painting's monotone back-ground. Smaller girls were stamping in the dust. The bird took up its song again, end-ing with a limp spray of fireworks; the lit-tle girls jumped at Isabelle's neck, dragged her off with them. I cursed her lightness, I cursed my seriousness. She was dissolving

away into a group, in a shrieking schoolyard. Of that walking corpse I could still
just see her rope of hair.

I was wandering alone around the lavatories. I went in. The air smelled midway
between the chemical odors of a sweet factory and of school disinfectant. I no longer
hated the efflux of disinfection that caught
in our throats those evenings we returned
to school. The smell was the backdrop to
our encounter. The wild children's screams
faded. A haze rose up from the frequently
scrubbed, light, wooden seat: the hazy tenderness of a mass of flaxen hair. I leaned
over the bowl. The still water reflected my
face before the creation of the world. I
touched the handle, the chain, I took my
hand away. The chain swung next to the
sad water. Someone called me. I didn't
dare to put the hook across and lock myself
in.

"Open the door," begged the voice.

Someone was rattling the doors.

I saw the eye that filled the hole cut high up in the lavatory door.

"My love."

Isabelle had come from the land of deluge, of upheaval, of crisis, of devastation. She was throwing me a liberated word, a plan, she was sending me the breath of the North Sea. I had the strength to say nothing and to be proud of it.

She is waiting for me but this is not safety. The word she said is too much. We watch each other, we are paralyzed.

I threw myself into her arms.

Her lips were seeking Thérèse in my hair, at my neck, in the folds of my apron, between my fingers, on my shoulder. Oh that I could multiply myself a thousand times and give her a thousand Thérèses. I am only myself. Too few. I am not a forest. A wisp of straw in my hair, a slip of confetti in the folds of my apron, a ladybird between my fingers, soft down on my neck, a scar on my cheek will flesh me out. Why am I not the crown of a willow for her hand caressing my hair?

I framed her face:

"My love."

I contemplated her, I was remembering her in this present, I had her beside me from last moment to last moment. When you are in love you are always on a railway platform.

"Are you here? Are you really here?"

I asked her questions, I demanded only silence. We chanted, we moaned, we discovered ourselves born actors. We squeezed each other until we nearly suffocated. Our hands were shaking, our eyes closed. We stopped, we began again. Our arms fell back, our inadequacy astonished us. I was shaping her shoulder; I wanted rustic caresses for her, I desired a rolling shoulder beneath my hand, a shell. She closed my fist, she was smoothing a stone. Tenderness blinded me. Forehead to forehead we told each other severely no. We clasped each other for last time after last time, we fused two tree trunks into one, we were the first and last lovers as we are the first and last mortals when we discover death. The cries, the roars, the noise of conversation in the schoolyard came in waves.

"Harder, harder . . . Squeeze me till I suffocate," she demanded.

I squeezed her but I did not stifle the cries, the courtyard, the boulevard, and its sycamores.

She freed herself, drew back, returned, she turned me into an armful of flowers, she threw me down, she said:

"Like that, it's like that . . ."

Her strength made me sad.

"But I want to hold you tight."

"You don't know how," she said.

Melancholy, Isabelle considered me.

I cast her against the lavatory door; I reeled against the cistern. She braced herself against the door, the hook fell at her feet. Already she was making up for my poor effort.

"Come back," she said.

She tipped her head to one side, she cooed to me slantways.

"Don't move. I see you," I said, lost in her.

I was plunging into her neck with my teeth, I was breathing in the darkness beneath her neckline: sycamore roots were shivering. I hold her tight, I stifle the tree, I hold her, I stifle the voices, I hold her, I banish the light.

"Is it true?"

"It's true," says Isabelle.

We watched the heart of blue sky through the hole in the door, we saw that the early morning sky was brooding over the earth.

Isabelle signaled that we were not looking at each other intensely enough. Love is excess. Our stares faltered, lost their way, resumed. I traced a student's shriek in Isabelle's eyes:

"I would like to eat you."

I pushed her against the wall, I pinned her hands down with my palms. My lashes fluttered in her lashes.

"It's incredible," she sighed.

My eyebrows brushed Isabelle's eyebrows.

"It's incredible the way I'm seeing you," she says.

We are talking. It's a shame. What is said is murdered. Our words that will not grow any bigger or any lovelier will wilt inside our bones.

I plunged into her eyes, I found clear water.

"I . . ."

Words wither feelings.

I put my hand over her mouth. Isabelle wanted to tell me.

"I . . ."

I was suffocating her while she wanted to confess. I lifted my hand from her mouth; her arms fell back.

"Don't be afraid. I will not say it."

She looked sorrowfully up at the sky in the heart-shaped hole. I had hurt her. We were lifted by the tempest of shrieks.

"Don't you understand?"

"I don't understand," says Isabelle.

"Whatever you wanted to tell me . . . you'll tell it later. Later."

She took my hands from around her waist. The sky was changing inside the heart: the lovely celluloid sky depressed us.

"It's too stupid. A moment ago we understood each other."

"Now we don't understand each other at all," says Isabelle.

Eyes closed, her virtuous twin spoke for her. I stepped back a pace, caught Isabelle's sweet silhouette. She emerged from a fading dream, the shouts from the courtyard piercing us through.

"Are you sulking?"

"I'm not sulking."

"Speak."

"No."

The statue will sink into the wall, will be absorbed by the lavatory wall.

"Are you leaving me?"

"I'm also waiting," she says.

Round fullness of her no spoken low, compressed beauty of the snowball in May that I'll neglect when I begin to die far away from gardens.

Secretly I gazed at the bituminous color of the still water. Isabelle raised an arm, pulled at the tortoiseshell pin in her coil of hair but did not draw it out. I was elated by her unfinished gesture. Isabelle had not opened her eyes. Her arm fell back, conquered by the lavatories' torpor.

I held her in my arms, with all the strength of my repentance, I breathed her in, I pressed her to my belly and she became my loincloth; I tottered with my darling embedded in me.

Isabelle was making my ankles drunk, rotting my knees with ecstasies. I was like a fruit stewed in her heat, I had the same liquorous seeping. Pincers softly tortured me. Her hairpin fell into the toilet bowl, we lost our balance. I plunged my hand into the water, fixed the pin back in her hair.

"I want that hand," she said.

Her cherishing was freezing me. I was parted from my hand which I no longer recognized. I reclaimed my hand, with my lips I dried her wet lips, I thrust my tongue into her mouth. Isabelle linked her hands together: she was creating an altar for my chin.

"My woman."

"Yes," replied my heart, a rose.

She told me to turn around, she wrapped her arms around me; she enthralled me, she used every resource. I was ashamed to turn my back to her. I would present her with a lumpish mass that I could not make slimmer. The blood rushed to my cheeks, my throat, as I was feeling for her tangled hair and crumpling her apron. Her hand was making my breathing uneven. I was sobbing without sound, without tears. Isabelle was sobbing too, pushing her hand down on my apron: my clothes were touching me. A shout from the schoolyard split through my chest; my heart began to beat down where the shout had been. A girl was practicing the piano, the rhyme she chanted reminding me of the cool drops scattered by a fountain in a park. My breath came evenly again.

"What time is it?" I ask.

"Recreation is extended. There won't be study hour today."

"I know. The time?"

I freed myself. She gave me a look of disdain.

"School can burn down for all I care."

"Me too. It can."

"While I couldn't care less if they expel me, I do care about losing you. Don't you understand?"

"Parted, that we will be," I say.

Isabelle threw herself on me. She was wrenching at my wrists:

"Parted, us? You're mad. Anyway, not before the summer holidays."

"You'll see. My mother, Isabelle, my mother . . ."

I stopped short.

"Your mother what?"

"She has to have me near her all the time . . ."

"They will not part us," said Isabelle.

Our lips were reconciled, the pleasure of our kiss went on.

Someone was rattling our door, entering the cubicle next to ours; they were not after us. Tip-tapping on the cement floor betrayed that the little girl had held on 'til the very last minute. She was pulling up her apron, her skirt, her petticoat. I closed my eyes, dispelled the hairless sex of this unknown child. The rags of my flesh fell upon lace. I opened my eyes, saw in Isabelle's that I had betrayed her for a flash of white knickers. The child relieved herself but we were embarrassed by the endless flow into the toilet bowl. I guessed this memory would stay with us. She slid off the seat, got to her feet, closed the door carefully.

"Speak Thérèse."

". . ."

I shall not allow you the nonsense you are after. Be quiet. Hold me tight. You are a village of five hundred souls, I am a village of five hundred souls. Hold tight, hold tight.

"Oh," I say, looking through the heart shape, "the girls have gone in. All of them . . ."

"Don't care. I'll say that I was ill and you, you'll think of something."

"What shall I think of?"

"A lie," said Isabelle.

"Weren't you ill in the refectory? I want to know."

"I told you."

That lock of hair will always be a mad slash above her eyes. Isabelle was kissing me all over. She was covering me with decorations, I overwhelming her with medals. The spring in her tangle was mingling with the spring in mine.

"I can't go on."

"I can't go on."

We weaken, we are dulling the sexes hidden beneath the tangle. Isabelle's head drops onto my shoulder. I have a falcon on my shoulder, I am the Grand Falconer.

"Enough," she says.

"You were saying that last night."

"We have to go out separately. I'll go first."

Only when I have set three embossed kisses on her apron belt.

"Keep this. It will be a link between us until tonight," said Isabelle.

She held out her arm, she unfastened her wristwatch for me.

A fly buzzes away; it's a departure. I see Isabelle walking away from the heart-shaped slot. The schoolyard dust has her feet, the tortoiseshell pins have her hair, the air possesses her lungs which I will not see, which I cannot hold against my breathing.

The concierge was ringing the first hour of lessons, the day students were running into the great courtyard, boarders slamming their locker doors, a little one bringing flowers to her teacher; the new monitor was questioning me in a corridor, thought I had been practicing scales in the music room, made me repeat the same lie, picking at her cotton gloves, clutching her packet of letter paper to her chest, she left to go into town, to the post offices, the park benches.

The concierge's arm rising, falling, ringing our return to school, setting our teeth on edge. A girl also asked me: Where were you? I said farewell to the monitor, to a friend—I had chosen my life—I slipped off in the direction of the study room. When I was bored—I was often bored for I did no work—I would open my desk and look through the labels on my rows of books; I felt that my lazy books were asleep on their feet like their owner. I had written the authors' names on the labels. I would cross my arms, listen for a long time, and in the end I would hear the murmuring of ancient tragedies.

"May lily!"

The few stems that made up the bouquet were lying on my leather pencil case. I could see a green and white crucifix, among leaves and flowers, laid out on my pencil case. The gift hardened me: I was too happy. I closed my desk again, locked my mind away deep inside, I returned to my desk. The bouquet had not vanished. She had given me flowers from a novel, she had left spear-tipped leaves and lucky May lily as one does when abandoning a child in a basket. I fled to the dormitory with my treasure.

I was walking on ocean currents, I advanced, taking care of my crystal feet, of the flowers in my fist. I went into Isabelle's box, I skipped the first hour of class for her. Her cell felt liberated, like my grandmother's bedroom the day they took away her coffin.

I want Isabelle. Let her come back, since the undertakers haven't snatched her from me. I wait for her within the four corners of this hearse, I breathe the smell of her bedspread, I wait for her with mourning in my breast. The headmistress will inspect the cells, will find me on Isabelle's bed, will expel me. We will be parted. I cannot leave her bed. I am trapped. What will we do tonight?

I made up a story of dizzy spells; I lied to the teacher, to the other girls; I slipped into the class, into the lesson; I made up more than necessary. I was thinking of Isabelle, I was tormenting myself behind my pile of books.

My mother gave in, but she gave in with bad grace. My mother has said it time and again, my mother will take me back before the holidays if she misses me, if she gets bored. If she were not married, I would be the one begging her: anything, anything you want but not to live far away from you in a school. Now it is the reverse. She is married. We are apart. How long will we remain apart? The time is over when I would scratch in the dirt for her, when I would slip through barbed-wire fences. I used to steal potatoes for us, from the fields. She took all my goods and chattels from me, even my satchel and lunch box. She sold our rabbits for a pittance—such a shame—eight days before her wedding. That was the end of

my meadows. I used to insist that I was her
fiancée. She would sigh. I didn't know what
exasperation looked like. She married without getting engaged. I scrubbed our three
steps but she wanted a merchant. I will not
be her daily laborer, I will not be her factory worker bringing in the money. She
sold the rag-and-bone man the ash drawer
from our stove, that I used to empty into
the henhouse while the first drops of coffee were falling in our cafetière, imitating
soft tongue-clicking sounds. Where are our
clothespins, our laundry blue? She threw it
all out. Mademoiselle was getting married.
She sold off everything. She has all she
requires. She is a married woman. I have
become a convent-school boarder: I have
no home. A man divided us. Hers. Your
mother would be so happy if you didn't
call me "Monsieur" . . . I shall always call
him "Monsieur." Another piece of bread,
Monsieur. No Monsieur, I don't like rare
meat. Call him "father," she says, after the

meal. Never. I prefer the refectory table where all our bread is shared. We thrust our hands into the bread basket, we do not say no thank you, yes please. I wandered about behind her: don't get married, don't get married . . . We would have done great things together: we would have been everything to each other. I would be cozy in her bed. She called me her little beggar; she would say: come nestle in my arms. She has a Louis XVI bed and she won't walk arm in arm with me anymore. Monsieur is between us. She wants a daughter and a husband. I have a demanding mother. I am locked up in a school, I don't walk behind them any longer on the evening promenade, I don't sleep in the room adjoining theirs any more. She wants me to swaddle her, she wants me to devote myself to her as soon as he has left. You are the only one in the world, I only love you in this world she tells me, but she has someone else. I have met Isabelle, I have someone too. I belong to Isabelle, I no longer belong to my mother.

At the blackboard a girl was drawing lines, crossing out triangles, writing the first letters of the alphabet next to the angles. I kept away from geometry.

What will we do in the night to come? Isabelle knows. Tomorrow, in this class, in front of this desk, I will know what we have done. I stare at the small *b*. I shall quickly recall what we did last night. Everything we did before she picks up the cloth, before she rubs out the small *b*. I cannot remember all the details. We didn't do anything. I am unfair. She kissed me, she came to me. Yes, she came. What a world . . . She came to lie upon me. I throw myself at Isabelle's feet. I can hardly remember what we did and it is all I can think about. What will we do tonight? Another girl rubs out the triangle, small *a*, small *b*, small *c*.

By four o'clock, my fever was mounting. Unleashed, the girls launched themselves into the corridors, their mouths full of soft white rolls.

I will come into the study room on tiptoe, I will drop my hand onto her shoulder, I will take her by surprise, I will whip her with my question. What will we do tonight?

I got there but I did not go in. People are working, officiating. I can hear the humming of their effort through the glass door, I am waiting for the right moment to appear, to play casual. I cannot see Isabelle there in supervised study. I shall enter like an invader. I entered like a felon.

"Quiet," said a girl, without raising her head.

It was stricter than in church. Isabelle was studying at the first table near the platform. I sat down in my place, opened a book to be like her; I kept watch, I counted one two three four five six seven eight. I cannot approach her, I cannot distract her. A girl went up to Isabelle's table and, without any hesitation, showed her an exercise. They were conversing, debating a point. Isabelle was living as she had lived before drawing me into her box. Isabelle was deceiving me, Isabelle fascinated me, Isabelle was starving me.

I cannot read now. The question recurs in each meander of the geography book. How can I use up the time? She turns her profile to me, she exposes herself, she does not know that I am drinking her in, she turns toward me, she will never know what she has given me. She speaks, she is far away, she works, she discusses: a colt gambols in her head. I am nothing like her. I will go to her, I will come between Isabelle and the other girl. She is yawning—she is so human—she pulls the pin from her twist of hair, pushes it back with the same gesture, her gesture in the lavatories. She knows what she will do tonight but she is not worried about it.

Isabelle leaned back over her work when

the girl left the study room. Isabelle had seen me.

I came down between the rows, squeezed tight by the walls of my joy.

"My love. You were there?" she said.

My head was empty.

"Bring your books over. We shall work together. It is stifling in here."

I opened the window and looked stoically out into the schoolyard.

"You're not bringing your books?"

"That's impossible."

"Why?"

"I could never work close to you. It is so strong . . ."

When she sees me and her face changes, it is genuine. When she does not see me and her face does not change that is genuine too.

"You really want me?" I ask.

"Sit down."

"I can't."

"My sweet."

"Don't call me my sweet. I am afraid."

"Sit down, let's talk."

"I can't talk anymore."

I sat down near her, I sobbed a soundless sob.

"What is it?"

"I can't explain."

She took my hand beneath the desk.

"Isabelle, Isabelle . . . What shall we do during recreation?"

"We'll talk."

"I don't want to talk." I took back my hand.

"Tell me what's wrong," Isabelle insisted.

"Don't you understand?"

"We will be together again. I promise you."

Toward seven in the evening, some girls gathered around me, suggested a stroll, some gossip. I faltered, I separated myself from them without acknowledging it. I was not free and no longer their age. I froze: Isabelle was tidying her books, she was close. The would-be truants and their temptations went off to another table. One tall girl standing alone before the open window was embroidering a handkerchief, her back to the sky. She raised her eyes, looked at me without seeing, she went on embroidering. I stayed at my desk. Isabelle was tidying her books yet the embroiderer was she.

My peach skin: the evening light in the playground at seven o'clock. My chervil: arachnean lace in the air. My sacred caskets: the trees' foliage with their breezy altars. What will we do tonight? The evening shades into the day, I see the evening in royal renaissance costume. The air cossets me but I don't know what we will do for our next night together. I hear noises, I hear seven-in-the-evening voices that embrace the thoughtful horizon. The glove of infinity has me in its grip.

"What are you looking at, Thérèse?"

"There . . . the geraniums . . ."

"What else?"

"The boulevard, the window—they're all you."

"Give me your arm. Don't you want to?"

The evening came upon us with its velvet mantle down to our knees.

"We can't go arm in arm. People will notice, we'll be caught."

"Are you ashamed?" asked Isabelle.

"Ashamed of what? Don't you understand? I am being careful." Groups of girls were watching us. Isabelle took my arm.

"Imagine you were expelled. It would be . . ."

I could not finish, I could not picture myself dead.

I tried again:

"You are the best student in the school. You won't be expelled. Imagine if I were."

"It would be dreadful," said Isabelle.

I shivered.

"Let's run!" she said.

Girls were waiting for the dinner bell in clusters by the walls and left the yard to us.

The schoolyard was ours. We ran, arms around each other's waist, our foreheads tearing through that lace in the air, we listened to the rippling of our hearts in the dust. Tiny white horses rode in our breasts. The girls and monitors laughed and clapped, they encouraged us when we began to slow.

"Faster, faster! Close your eyes. I'm leading," said Isabelle.

There was a wall to put behind us. We would be alone.

"You're not running fast enough. Yes, yes . . . Close your eyes, close your eyes."

I obeyed.

Her lips brushed my lips.

"I'm afraid of falling over and killing myself," I said.

I opened my eyes: we were alive.

"Afraid? I'm guiding you," she said.

"We can run more if you want."

I was exhausted.

"My woman, my child," she said.

She gave and she withheld words. She could hug them to her while hugging me. I half-released my fingers from around her waist, I counted: my love, my woman, my child. Three fingers for my three engagement rings.

A girl was ringing the dinner bell.

"Keep on ringing," called Isabelle to her.

Drowned in her ringing, the ringer laughed.

"One more run," pleaded Isabelle. "I must talk to you, I must tell you about it."

"Talk to me?"

I thought there would be no more nights. We were running but I was paralyzed. I took the lead:

"Am I not to come?"

The bell was ringing long and loud.

"You will come tonight," said Isabelle.

It seemed that the ringer was ringing differently and that our wedding was beginning on the church steps, once the other couples had been blessed.

"Louder, louder," called Isabelle to the ringer.

"Enough, enough!" Shouted the play-ground monitor. The girl hooked the chain back on its nail.

We walked in step, through the resounding throng. We were severe, shackled, we were an official couple without past, without future, we had cast-iron crowns upon our heads, bailiff's chains across our chests, our majesty was conferred by the weight of our finery, we proceeded with our wrists gripped in our identical uniforms.

A convent bell rang in another world.

We shuffled into rows.

"Speak again."

"No, since it's over," said Isabelle.

The ringing of the bell faded away: the convent was drowning in the general shipwreck, the girls fell silent for the minute of silence. Isabelle changed places. We closed ranks, we kept our distance and the embroiderer embroidered among the troops.

"I love you."

"I love you," I said too.

The little ones were already eating. We ignored the words we had just exchanged, we each chatted to the girl on the other side, we sought refuge in these distractions.

My neighbor on the right was embroidering something under the table.

"Who's that for?"

"That question again!" she exclaimed. "For my brother. Do you like the pattern?"

"You have a brother?"

"Do you like the pattern?"

"How old is he?"

"Eighteen. A year older than me. It's he who will get me out of here. We shall never leave each other."

"You know that already?"

"When we've finished our studies we

shall run a family hotel together at the sea-side. We have the money . . ."

"Do you look much like him?"

"I'm the very image of him as a girl. Why were you running so fast with Isabelle?"

"Why won't you ever leave your brother?"

The servants were bringing in the dishes, my neighbor put away her needlework. I ate as old people do: alone with my plate. Isabelle rested her elbow on the book she had taken from me while we were running in the yard.

Dusk was falling as crepe falls over faces. I wanted to lay my body on Isabelle's, I wished we could go up to the dormitory. But she was thinking, huddled in the folds of her stony white apron. There she was, my museum, there the snag in the crepe. I languished, I was deadly, the big cats' stalking slowed the routes through my favorite landscapes, the refectory clock's stilted time wanted persuasion. The unpredictable breeze swept in, it caressed my hands, seduced my memories.

How secret our separation was, in the general evening separation, when we all scattered at the dormitory door.

As ever, I was back at my percale curtain. An iron hand snatched me away, steered me elsewhere. Isabelle threw me onto her bed and buried her face in my underpants, in my crotch.

"Come back when they are asleep," she said.

She drove me away, she fascinated me.

I was in love: I had nowhere to hide. I should have only waiting rooms and the time suspended between our meetings. I dropped onto my bed.

"I didn't hear a noise," said the monitor. "What are you doing? Not yet undressed!"

"I was lying down. I was thinking about my work," I say.

"You must get undressed. Quickly now. I'm turning out the lights."

The curtain fell closed again, Isabelle coughed.

Isabelle was coughing, sitting up in bed. Isabelle was ready with her cape of hair over her shoulders. Her cape. Returning to this scene paralyzed me. I collapsed onto her chair, onto the rug: the scene followed me everywhere. The monitor had turned out the lights.

"I'm dying to get to sleep," said a girl at the far end of the dormitory.

"Shush," retorted the new monitor.

The dormitory settled.

I was undressing in the darkness, pressing my chaste hand to my skin, I was breathing myself in, recognizing myself, abandoning myself. I packed the silence down into my washbasin; wringing out my wash sponge, I was wringing out the silence too; drying myself, I smoothed it along my skin.

The monitor turned the light out in her room; a girl was muttering; Isabelle coughed again: she was calling me. I decided that if I did not close the box of dental paste, I would remember this atmosphere, of before I returned to Isabelle and her box. I was creating a past for myself.

"Are you ready?" whispered Isabelle, behind my curtain.

She was gone again. Her discretion delighted and disappointed me.

Once again I opted for the regulation nightgown, which I now put on; I calculated too that I would change what I wore every evening, that a day student could give my dresses to a laundry in town.

I opened the window in my cell. The night and the sky needed nothing of us. Living in the open air would be sacrilege. Only our absence could further ornament the trees' evening. I dared a quick look into the passage but the passage was disheartening. Their sleep frightened me: I hadn't the courage to step over the sleeping girls, to walk barefoot over their faces. I closed the window and, like the leaves, the percale quivered.

"Are you coming?"

I turned on the light: her hair did indeed fall like a cape as I had pictured it, but I hadn't foreseen the sturdy tautness of her nightgown. Isabelle stepped away again.

I came in with my flashlight, which I held as you hold a missal.

"Take off your clothes," said Isabelle.

She was leaning on one elbow, her hair raining down over her profile.

"Take off your dress, turn out the light."

I turned out her hair, her eyes, her hands. I shed my nightgown. This was not new: I was casting off the lovers' first night.

"What are you doing?" said Isabelle.

"Dawdling."

"Come!"

"Yes Isabelle, yes."

She was growing restless in bed while I, in my shyness, was posing naked for the shadows.

"But what are you up to?"

I slipped into her bed. I had been cold, I would be warm.

I stiffened, I didn't want to crush her pubic hair. She forced me, she laid me down along her body; Isabelle wanted the union of our skins. I was reciting my body upon hers, bathing my belly in the lilies of her belly, finding my way inside a cloud. She skimmed my hips, she shot strange arrows. I rose up, I fell back onto her.

"We must not move, not breathe. Be dead," she said.

We were listening to what was happening inside us, emanating from us. Couples surrounded us, spying.

The springs creaked.

"Careful!" She said, at my mouth.

The monitor had switched on the light in her room.

I was kissing the mouth of a vanilla-scented little girl. We had turned good again.

"Let's hug each other," said Isabelle.

We tightened the circle of our hold.

"Crush me . . ."

She wanted to but she couldn't. She was thrashing my pelvis.

"Don't listen to her," she said.

The monitor was urinating in her chamber pot.

"She will go back to sleep," I said.

Isabelle rubbed her toe against my instep, a sign of friendship.

"She's gone back to sleep," said Isabelle.

"If she was listening for us . . ."

"She's a pain."

I met Isabelle's mouth with mine; I was afraid of the monitor; I drank down our saliva. It was an orgy of dangers. We had had darkness in our mouths and in our throats, we knew that peace had returned.

"Press me down," she said.

"The springs . . . they'll squeak . . . we'll be heard."

We were talking among the dense foliage of summer nights.

I was pressing, blotting out myriads of alveoli.

"Am I heavy?"

"You will never be heavy. I'm a little cold," she said.

My fingers saw her wan shoulders. I flew away, with my beak I picked up wisps of wool caught in thorny hedges, I laid them around Isabelle's shoulders. I was drumming on her bones with my downy hammers, my kisses tumbled down one after the other, I launched into an avalanche of tenderness. My hands relieved my tired lips: I molded the sky around her shoulder. Isabelle sat up, she took my wrists, she fell back down and I fell with her into the hollow of her shoulder. My cheek rested in a contour.

"My treasure."

I was talking to the broken outline.

"Yes," said Isabelle.

She said, "I'm coming," but hesitated.

"I'm coming," Isabelle said again.

She tied her hair back, her elbow swept over my face. I waited.

A hand came to rest on my neck: a winter sun whitened my hair. The hand was tracing veins, downward. The hand stopped. My pulse was beating against Isabelle's hand, its mount of Venus. The hand climbed again: it drew widening circles, it dropped away into nowhere, it was extending the waves of sweetness around my left shoulder while my right shoulder on the pillow was abandoned to the night striated with the other girls' breathing. I was learning the velvet nap of my bones, the aura of my flesh, the infinities in my shapes. The hand was lingering, bringing dreams of lawn shawls. The sky pleads charity when your shoulder is caressed: the sky was pleading. The hand was climbing back, fixing a wimple of velour up to my chin, the persuasive hand descending again, pressing, replicating curves. In the end it was the pressure of friendship. I took Isabelle in my arms, I quivered with gratitude. I smoothed her hair, she smoothed mine.

"Can you see me?" asked Isabelle.

"I can see you. I want to give too."

"Listen!"

". . ."

"No, nothing . . . They're sleeping and those who aren't won't tell on us."

"I want to give you . . ."

She cut me short, she slipped under the covers, she kissed my short curls.

"Horses," a girl cried out.

"Don't be frightened. She's dreaming. Give me your hand," said Isabelle.

I was crying with joy.

"What's wrong? Turn on the light."

"No, don't. No, no . . ."

"But you're crying?" she asked, alarmed.

"I love you: I'm not crying."

I dried my eyes.

The hand undressed my arm, stopped near the vein, around the crook of my elbow, grew promiscuous among its patterns, followed them down to the wrist, to the tips of the nails, resleeved my arm in a long suede glove, fell from my shoulder like an insect, perched at my armpit, rubbed at the tuft of hair. My face tensed, I listened to my arm as it answered the adventurer. Willing persuasion, the hand brought my arm, my armpit, into the world. The hand wandered over the babbling of white bushes, over the last frosts on the prairies, over the first buds' oozing. Spring, which had been chirruping with impatience inside my skin, burst out in lines, in curves, in parabolas. Stretched out on the darkness, Isabelle was tying ribbons around my feet, unfolding the binding of my turmoil. Hands flat on the mattress, I was carrying out the same spellbinding labor as she. She would kiss what she had caressed, then, with her light hand, she would ruffle and flick with her feather duster of perversity. The octopus in my guts was quivering, Isabelle was drinking at my right breast, at my left. I was drinking with her, I suckled on shadows when her mouth moved away. The fingers returned, encircling, weighing the breast's warmth; the fingers finished in my belly, hypocritical wrecks. A tribe of slaves all sharing Isabelle's face was fanning my forehead, my hands.

She knelt on the bed:

"Do you love me?"

I led the hand up to those rare tears of joy.

Her cheek wintered between my thighs. I turned my flashlight on her, saw her fanned-out hair, saw my belly raining silk. The flashlight slipped, Isabelle veered into a new tack.

We seemed to be marrying with fangs in our skin, horsehairs in our hands: we were reeling on the teeth of a rake.

"Harder, harder," she said.

We bit each other, we thrashed at the shadows.

We slowed, we came back with our plumes of smoke, with black wings at our heels. Isabelle leapt out of the bed.

I wondered why Isabelle was redoing her hair.

With one hand she laid me down flat on the bed, with the other she tormented me with the yellow light.

I hid behind my arms:

"I'm not pretty. You're intimidating me," I said.

She saw our future in my eyes, she was looking an instant ahead, she was keeping it in her blood.

She got back into bed, she lusted for me with gold-sifter's fingers.

I was flattering her; I preferred failure to preparations. Making love with her mouth was enough for me: I was afraid and I called for help with my finger stumps. Two fine paintbrushes were wandering among my folds. My heart was beating in a mole-hill, my head was full of compost. Suddenly everything changed. Two alternating fingers were attending on me. How masterly her caress, how inevitable her caress . . . Closed, my eyes were listening: the finger grazed my pearl, the finger waited. I wanted to be capacious, to help it.

The regal and diplomatic finger was advancing, withdrawing, choking me, beginning to enter, offending the octopus deep inside, bursting the cloud of unease, stopping, starting up, waiting close to viscera. I was clenching, I enclosed the flesh of my flesh, its marrow and its vertebrae. I rose and fell back again. The finger that had not hurt me, the finger come in gratitude came out. The flesh ungloved it.

"Do you love me?" I asked.

I was hoping for confusion.

"You mustn't shout," said Isabelle.

I crossed my arms over my face, I listened beneath my eyes squeezed tight.

Two fingers entered, two pirates. Isabelle was tearing open and beginning the deflowering. They were oppressing me; they wanted, my flesh did not want.

"My love . . . You're hurting me." She put her hand over my mouth.

"I won't complain," I said.

The gag was a humiliation.

"It hurts. It must. It hurts . . ."

I gave myself to the night and without wanting to I helped the fingers.

"You can, you can . . ."

I leant forward so as to tear myself, to make Isabelle's fingers crack, to be closer to her face, to be near my injured sex: she threw me onto the pillow.

She was pounding, pounding, pounding . . . We could hear loud slaps of flesh on flesh. She was putting out the virgin eye.

I was in pain: I was approaching freedom but I couldn't see what was happening.

We listened to the sleeping girls, we sobbed for breath. Her fingers had left a line of fire.

"Let's rest," she said.

My recollection of the two fingers grew sweeter, my swollen flesh began to recover, bubbles of love rose up. But Isabelle was there again, the fingers turned faster and faster. Where had this mounting wave come from? Smooth wrappings inside my knees. My heels were drugged, my visionary flesh was dreaming.

"I can't go on."

"Quiet."

I lost myself with her in this tender gymnastics.

The fingers were too short, the knuckles were obstructing our fever, the knuckles would go no further.

"I want to," Isabelle grieved.

The springs creaked, again we could hear each slap of flesh.

"You're hot."

"I want, I want you!"

Isabelle crashed into my arms. The sweat running down her face, her hair, her throat, wet my face, my hair, my throat. Her last gift after the deflowering.

"You're calling me? You want me?" Isabelle asked.

She returned again, obeying already and to the point of paroxysm.

The fingers' whirling reached as far as my languid knees but they did not bring the unearthly wave I was expecting. The pleasure was approaching. It was only an echo. The slow fingers left me. I was greedy for her presence.

"Your hand, your face . . . Come closer."

"I'm tired."

Make her come, make her lend me her shoulder or indeed let her borrow mine, make it so her face is near mine. I must trade my innocence for hers. She is out of breath: she is resting. I have to move to hear her living. Isabelle coughed as if she were coughing in a library.

I sat up with infinite care, I felt completely new. My sex, my meadow.

"Say good night to me."

Isabelle jumped.

"Say good night . . ."

I turned the light on. I had seen the blood, I had seen my reddened hair. I turned it off.

She sat up on her knees in the bed and, naturally, I presented my curly-haired nest so she could bury her face in it. What could I say to her while her cheek was cradled there? She was spoiling me.

"I want to give," I said.

"Be quiet."

"I want to give."

I turned the light on, looked down at my reddened hair.

"I'm ashamed," I said.

"Ashamed of what?"

"Of the blood."

"You're silly."

I went up to the curtain, I crossed one leg over the other, I posed, I turned the light on myself. I was naked: I wanted to be artificial.

"You're upsetting me," said Isabelle.

She stood up.

She was coming. She was hiding her face in her hands, her hair flowing down all on one side.

"Oh."

I welcomed her into my arms. With my teeth I picked the dried blood from under her fingernails. I put her to bed.

I laid my little girl down, I lifted her head, patted the pillow, smoothed, freshened the bed.

"You are looking after me," said Isabelle.

I was warming her foot on my breast. Isabelle was giving me a child. Now we would be making love, now I would be lay-ing him back in the cradle. I have never wanted children other than the people I have loved. For me, they were love.

"I'm going, Isabelle."

She was holding me back by the hips, with all her strength.

"I'll scream if you go."

I stayed.

"More supple," she said to the hand that was no longer mine, that she was guiding.

I entered the old refuge.

"You're nodding off," she said.

My finger was dreaming, I was quietly wandering.

She put her arm on mine, I tingled with pleasure as our arms met.

You have to remove yourself in order to give. I wanted to become a machine that was not mechanical. My life was her pleasure. I looked beyond Isabelle, I was working inside the belly of the night. We drew into accord as we vanished together. The moan. She sat up, she frightened me. Already the shadow of that pleasure, already. Was she dying or indeed living? The rhythm would tell. I followed everything in her; with my mind's eye I could see the light in her flesh. In my head there was another Thérèse, her legs open, thrown up to the sky, receiving all that I was giving to Isabelle.

"Come and rest," she said.

I became a child again.

Living, stretched out, floating, parted, in contemplation, we could believe in eternal rest. The brook of solitude was so cool:

"I want to tell you . . ."

"You're happy. Don't question it," said Isabelle.

We had put our nightgowns back on.

I said:

"What are you thinking?"

"I'm just living. And you?"

"I was listening to your heart. Such a prison . . . Are you listening to it too?"

"I don't feel sad," said Isabelle.

I turned to face her:

"You're not sleeping?"

"I was seeing us in a cinema. I was misbehaving, not being good," said Isabelle.

"In a cinema . . . That is strange . . . It's possible that reminds me of something. Yet it isn't a memory. It's as if I had been to this cinema that I don't know," I said.

"It won't happen. We aren't free," said Isabelle.

"Let's run away."

"I've no money."

"Me neither. We'll sell what can be sold, then we'll take the train, let's try. We won't starve to death."

"We shan't run away. We have to be here. We can have every night to ourselves if we are careful. Do you hate the school?"

"Not at all. I'm afraid they'll make me leave . . . Will you see me between your classes? Say, will you see me?"

She didn't reply.

Two rosettes became one.

"Who told you?"

"I've always known," said Isabelle.

"I'm hungry."

She opened the drawer in her night table, without looking away she pushed a bar of dusty chocolate into my mouth.

"Eat," said Isabelle, "eat and calm down."

My cheek bumped against the flashlight on the pillow.

One after the other I lit up the palms of her hands, far from our union.

"I need you," I said.

"I need you," said Isabelle.

"Yes. Yes," I moaned.

"Someone's there," said Isabelle, calmly.

She stood up, looked out into the passage.

"No one. No one was there," said Isabelle.

She leaned over the bed. Isabelle was not going to lie down again.

She was frolicking between my thighs,

she drew alarming figure eights, drawing them bigger and bigger, she was stroking as she bent over me.

Three fingers entered, three guests that my flesh swallowed up.

So she came back to bed, like the acrobat bending low who carries his partner balanced on his fingertip.

"You aren't listening to me," said Isabelle.

"I'm listening. You're telling me little things, you have come back, you are inside me. The rain . . . Oh, yes . . . yes! I don't hate it. It's a friend. Yes, yes . . . Let's die together, Isabelle, die while you are me and I am you. I'll stop thinking that we will be parted. Let's die, don't you think?"

"I don't want to. I want this. I want to be deep inside you. Dying . . . that's too stupid."

"If I had leprosy would you abandon me?"

"I don't have it, you don't have it, we haven't got it. Why are you turning the light on?"

Isabelle took her hand away, she crossed her arms over her face.

"Would you leave me?"

She shrugged.

"Look at me," I said.

"I'm looking with my eyes closed."

"If I were to die tomorrow would you stay alive?"

She turned to me. She appeared within a frost-edged bramble each time she turned around like this.

"You would stay alive. You're not answering."

Isabelle pressed her hands together. Impulses, twitches were flying across her face: her spirit was in ferment.

"It's a difficult question," said Isabelle.

She would not open her eyes.

"Answer!"

"These questions are too big."

Isabelle lifted her eyes. Now she was staring at me:

"Do you really want to die with me when you say that? Truly? You would really like us to die at the same time?"

Isabelle threw back her head. She was thinking hard.

"I don't know anymore," I said.

"Give me your hand," she said. "No . . . don't give me your hand. Not now."

"You are so beautiful . . . I really would like to but I couldn't. I can't imagine you dead. You're so beautiful . . ."

"Think about us. Could you?"

"I don't know, I don't know anymore. It is good to be alive. And you? What about you?"

"Yet if we don't want to be parted," said Isabelle.

"You could?"

"We shall have to come around to it," said Isabelle. "You couldn't now, but I'm not cross with you. I never thought I would

ask that of you. From a cliff . . . one night
. . . together . . ."

"It's awful, what you're saying."

"How easily you frighten! With you, it
wouldn't scare me."

"Don't think about it, Isabelle."

"I told you: these questions are too
big."

"You are beautiful. I don't want to lose
you."

Isabelle turned back to the partition but
I said it again into her hair, to her eyes, that
she was beautiful. She hated the tinsel of
cheap compliments. She closed up, she was
far away.

"Lie down, take up the whole space. Be
beautiful," I said.

Isabelle straightened:

"Listen: it's three in the morning. I
don't want to leave you."

She clung to my neck. The night had
betrayed us. I adored all that was vulnerable.

"Take the flashlight. I'll do your hair. Would you like me to?"

She shrugged, indulgent:

"Do you hear? It's raining."

It was only the last sighs of a soft-hearted night.

I picture her face in fantasy: her hair tumbles down over her shoulders but she is not wretched. Her little nose will never grow old. The earthworms will be sated but her little nose will never change. This will be the tomb's treasure, this is the perfect little bone. How austere her straight little nose is.

"What's wrong with me, what are you looking at?"

"Nothing."

I didn't dare talk to her about her immortality. She took my hand, she laid her cheek in it.

"Let me fix you."

Isabelle was happy to give herself to me:

"What are you doing with me?"

"I'm putting flowers on you."

"You do know this is serious?" Isabelle said.

"I'm not playing."

"But it's not real. We mustn't waste our time."

"You are lovely and I'm making you lovelier."

"I won't have you make an idol of me."

I saw the scintillation of my tears. I did not cry.

"What have I done to you, tell me what I've done to you," I begged. "I wanted to ornament you . . ."

"That's all?" asked Isabelle.

"That's all."

But I loved her with crepe bows on every finger. She sat up in the bed:

"I know it: we will be parted," she said.

I gathered up the bedspread, I struggled with the bolster.

We had created this celebration of obliv-

ion to time. We hugged to us all the Isa-
belles and the Thérèses who would be in
love after us, with other names; we ended
up clutching each other in the midst of
creakings and tremblings. We had rolled,
entwined, down a slope of darkness. We
had stopped breathing to bring a stop to
life and a stop to death.

I broke into her mouth as one goes
to war: I was hoping I would ransack her
entrails and mine.

The note of a whistle, a train, a station,
but the silence remained, weighing on our
heads. Isabelle put her hair on my shoulder.

"Are you sleepy?"

"I'm not sleepy."

She mumbled it.

Something came away from my hip, fell
upon the mattress: a hand. Isabelle was
asleep. The dawn would be our dusk, from
one minute to the next.

My face brushed against hers.

"Don't sleep."

The dawn, ever punctual when something somewhere is dying, lay waiting with her trailing chiffons. Small boats could be seen heaving themselves clear of the reeds.

"Don't sleep . . ."

I prized the hand away from its ringlets, I listened out across my kingdom. Her sleeping excited me. I planted my eight-year-old, little girl's lips on her pale lips, I betrayed Isabelle with Isabelle herself, I cheated her of the kiss that I was giving her. She awoke at my mouth:

"You're there?"

She was talking: she was bringing me the finest of the shadows where she had been resting. I was breathing the sulphurous haze of her presence.

"You want to?"

"Yes," said Isabelle.

We skimmed and flew over our shoulders with the wild fingers of autumn. We hurled great striations of light into nests, we fanned caresses, we wove patterns out of the sea breeze, we wrapped our legs in zephyrs, we held the hum of taffeta in our palms. Entering was so easy. Our flesh was in love with us, our scent sprayed up. Our leavening, our bubbles, our bread. The back and forth was not servitude but back and forth of beatitude. I was losing myself in Isabelle's finger as she was losing herself in mine. How our conscientious fingers dreamed . . . What weddings of movement. Clouds helped us. We were streaming with light.

The wave came on reconnaissance, it intoxicated our feet, it swept through again. Lianas were released, a clarity grew within our ankles. The unfurling sweetness was complete. My knees crumbled to ashes.

"It's too much. Tell me it's too much."

"Be quiet."

"I can't be quiet, Isabelle."

I was kissing her shoulder, giving myself up to the shipwreck once more.

"Speak."

"I can't," said Isabelle.

"Open your eyes."

"I can't," said Isabelle.

"What are you thinking about?"

"You."

"Speak, speak."

"Aren't you happy?"

"Look . . . No, don't look."

"I know. Soon it will be light. Close your eyes, ward it off," said Isabelle.

The sun was rising, Isabelle was falling asleep again.

I was yawning in the wet and milky meadows, I demanded help and protection from the sleeper, possessor of the dark night whose passing I lamented. In her head my sleeper held night that could never come to an end, in her heart my sleeper held the song of the unsleeping nightingale. I breathed lightly, I was barely alive next to her.

She was embracing me, she did not forget her anxiety while sleeping:

"You're not asleep."

"I'm asleep. Sleep."

A few girls turned over: the dawn was shimmering in their dreams.

I got up and Isabelle got up too. I went out into the passage but she dragged me roughly back into her cell.

She opened her gown, she showed me her pride, she made me sore with her thigh between my thighs. I wanted to go. Her sleep had made me desperate.

"Don't go!"

Isabelle collapsed:

"Why did I sleep, why?"

She was shaking.

Too much love wearies.

"Do what you would like to do," I said.

She licked, she scented the night's residues on my face, she kneeled.

Her face found its way, it was exploring me. Lips saw and touched what I would not see. I was humiliated for her. Indispensable and neglected, so I was with my face far from Isabelle's face. Her damp forehead troubled me. A saint was licking my stains. Her gifts impoverished me. She was giving too much of herself: I was guilty.

"Go and rest. There's one girl studying already," Isabelle said.

I obeyed. I threw myself into the river of sleep.

"I hope we find you quite awake now," said the monitor. I was asleep on my feet.

"The relative propositions may consequently indicate different circumstantial relationships . . ."

Isabelle was saying this to someone else. Isabelle was already tidying her box.

I woke up properly, dressed with care, ready for her greeting. She came in with a whirlwind's scorn while I was smoothing brilliantine through so as to be like a precious bloom.

"Hello."

"Hello."

We could not look at each other.

"It's a fine day."

"Yes, it's a fine day."

But the sun was being hoisted over us. We looked down.

"Are you ready?" asked Isabelle.

"No. You can see that."

Her name, which I was avoiding, my saliva, which I could not swallow . . .

"Would you like me to help you?"

"No."

"I would like my watch back," said Isabelle.

"Of course. Your watch . . ."

I fussed around the night table.

"Put it on my wrist," said Isabelle.

We saw each other again, we looked once more with the eyes of our night.

"Please, put my bracelet on."

"Tell me if I make it too tight."

"It's easy. There's a mark."

"Can't you do it?" Isabelle asked.

"I can," I said.

"Your voice has gone," she said.

"Has it? Will you excuse me? I must finish tidying up."

I tossed the lid of the washbasin onto the floor, I emptied the basin.

"Too much racket in there," said the monitor.

"Don't file your nails in here. Don't file your nails . . ."

"Why not?" asked Isabelle.

"Not here. Not now."

"But you're dusting . . ."

"Don't file your nails. Stop."

Isabelle opened the window in my cell.

"You threw out your filings?"

"You didn't like it," said Isabelle.

I put away the soap, I cleaned the porcelain dish where I kept my toothbrush.

Isabelle is ready to stab me. This idea ran through me while I was putting away the towels and sponges on the towel rail. I was expecting the bite of a knife.

"Did the monitor see you come in?" Isabelle did not want to reply.

I took up the honeycomb towel again, I dried the tooth-glass.

"Does she know you are here?"

Suddenly she pulled my hair. She plunged her dagger into the nape of my neck.

"Someone's coming," Isabelle said.

Isabelle tore herself from her task. She edged the curtain aside, she slipped out.

"False alarm. No one's in the passage," said Isabelle. She reassured me. She had vanished.

But the monitor had come:

"There was someone in here with you. Don't deny it. Your friend's name?"

"Friend?" I said contemptuously.

"Why are you smirking?"

"Isabelle was helping me. She helps me when I am slow. Our old monitor knew that."

"You surprise me. I thought you two did not get on. Hurry along then, hurry, we're going downstairs," said the monitor relieved by my words.

Andréa, a half boarder who used to come in early, who lunched with us in the refectory but dined and slept in the country, spent her Thursdays and Sundays looking out on a meadow, beside a stable. Andréa made charming winter quarters. Her eyes shone with cold, the ice melting her always-chapped lips. I would shake her hand; I was touching the oxygen of freedom.

"Is it sunny over your way?" I would ask.

"The weather's the same as here," she would reply.

"No more frosts?" I would ask, out of nostalgia for the white frosts.

"The frosts are over. My father is sharpening his scythe for the harvest," she said.

That morning, I left Andréa to her white frosts.

"Renée was showing me some photographs. What do you think of this one?" Isabelle asked me before we went into the refectory.

"It's a landscape, nicely done."

Isabelle was making overtures while her hair mingled with mine.

I was afraid I would scream. I stepped backward.

Isabelle threw back her lock of hair, stepped forward. Her cheek pressed a long kiss on mine.

"Stop, I say, stop, you are killing me."

She pushed me, furiously, into Renée, excused herself.

Younger girls disturbed us with their shouts. I love you and you won't answer me, said the hand resting in mine. Renée was gazing at the photograph, guessing, probably, at the couple next to her, for she dared not look up. I was caught between the false innocence of the one and the other's audacity. Isabelle's hand, through the folds in her apron, was stroking me. It was crazy. I was rotting away, my flesh was bursting ripe.

"You can give back the photograph at the end!" said Renée.

"Leave it. She's examining it," said Isabelle to Renée.

Guessing that the glazed paper was my protection, Isabelle fended off the lightning that would have struck right through me, that would have revealed the terrifying halo in my belly. I collapsed, clutching the landscape in my hand.

"Slap her," Renée said to Isabelle; "slap her, she'll recover."

Isabelle did not reply.

"A handkerchief, quick a handkerchief, eau de cologne," shouted someone else. "Thérèse has collapsed . . . Thérèse is ill."

"Find some vinegar, find some spirit!"

I was listening and resting on the tiles while simulating a dead faint to follow my collapse. I dared not get to my feet for fear of ridicule. I am often exhausted on waking up: I imagine the sorrow, I imagine the absence of sorrow of those finding out that I had ceased to live. Isabelle was still silent, Isabelle was getting used to my death. Girls were shaking me, peering under my eyelids, calling my name; I was not there. I had disappeared because I could not love her in public: the scandal I had spared us would fall upon me alone. I stood up, avoiding the horrid smell of vinegar.

"It was nothing," I said.

I patted my forehead.

"Go up to the dormitory," said the new monitor. "Who will go with her?"

She dabbed at my forehead, my lips, with her cursed vinegar.

"I'll go," said Isabelle.

We left, a sorry pair, and heard the military step of the girls going into the refectory. Isabelle was embracing a girl who had had a fainting spell. The wretchedness is greater than the fault. We walked without speaking, without looking at each other. She stopped when I stopped, she walked when I started to walk again. I tramped sadly over the mat at the foot of the stairs, I hoped for reconciliation. She . . . I loved her all along the banisters, at every step. Every time I lifted a foot I made a vow of reconciliation. She withdrew her arm, buttoned her smock up at the wrist, put her arm around my waist again, to comply with the monitor's order. It was a nurse who sent me down the dormitory passage, who lifted the curtain to my cell, who went off to her own room. My smock sprayed with vinegar, my wet hair, were disheartening.

She opened the curtain wide, she aired everything before coming in. She would disinfect my soul; she was intimidating me.

"Why did you do that?"

She addressed me like family, she was honeying our past.

"Why did you do that?"

". . ."

"Did you fake it or were you really tired?"

"I faked it. Don't scold me."

"I'm not scolding you."

"Leave that brush alone! Don't go . . ."

She came back into my box and the sun presented her to me. I gave her hand my deepest kiss.

"Forgive me," I pleaded.

"Don't. It's awful, what you're saying. Are you tired?"

"I won't be tired until the holidays."

"I must be seen in the refectory, Thérèse."

Her weight on my knees was comforting.

"Close your eyes, listen: I collapsed in the hall because you were getting too close. My strength vanished. You were provoking me."

"It's true," said Isabelle.

She opened her eyes: our soft kiss made us moan.

"Someone's coming," said Isabelle. "The saliva . . . wipe away the saliva . . ."

"Not yet at table, Isabelle!" exclaimed the head monitor. "As for you, I'll have your breakfast brought up here."

When I returned to the study room, I found an envelope inside my locker. I sat down in Isabelle's place, since I had no lesson to attend; I contemplated the ink splots on her desk. A few girls were studying in the light of the new day. The white envelope rustled when I touched my hand to my heart; Isabelle's writing shivered. I put off reading it, I studied a physics textbook, I worked halfheartedly inside my idler's carapace. The sun was tempting me, the sky's brightness was tinting my wrists; through the open windows, the teachers' pompous voices had lost the resonance lent them by winter classrooms.

Seasons, give us your rags. Let us be wanderers with our hair slicked down by rain. Isabelle, would you . . . would you set up home with me beside an embankment? We would devour our crusts like lions, we seek out the piquancy of the gales; we would have a house, lace curtains, while the caravans are passing, heading for the borders. I would undress you in the corn, I would shelter you inside haystacks, I would lie with you in the water beneath the low branches, I would care for you upon the forest mosses, I would take you in the alfalfa fields, I would raise you up on the hay wains, my Carolingian lady.

I escaped from the study room, I read her letter in the lavatories:

"Gather strength, sleep when you can, fortify yourself for the night to come, think of our future from this evening."

I wound the chain of the flush around my neck; with each link, I kissed the next of Isabelle's vertebrae. I tore up her instructions and threw them into the lavatory bowl. Quarter past nine. The clock in the great court marked an Olympian time, higher than the narrow time of the classrooms.

My physics book's paper cover tore off, my retractable pencil rolled away beneath the radiator: the things I was leaving behind were fleeing from me. Outside in the corridor, day students were waiting for the second class, they were coming and going behind the glass door. They were not in love: their ease and their nonchalance oppressed me.

"You're being spoken to," said a girl.

I was sleeping during the cosmography class.

"She's been ill," said the girl. "She fainted in the hall. We don't know what's wrong with her."

I went back to sleep.

After cosmography came ethics, through which I also dozed. Eleven twenty-five, eleven thirty, eleven thirty-five. I could see our reunion in the broad angle of that eleven thirty-five. My awaking had been that of an undisciplined sentry. I powdered my face beneath my desk lid; in my powder compact mirror I discovered what Isabelle would love and what she would not. The bell was ringing, pupils roaring, I had a plan.

"Yes, two roses . . . two red roses. Go to the best florist . . ."

"What size?" asked the day student.

"Whichever are the prettiest. Yes, if you like: for a teacher. Smell them before you buy. Pink roses, ideally."

"Leave me to it," said the day student, "you can count on me."

Other day students were slashing at my face with their scarves, their gloves; they were pushing me, dragging me toward the forbidden gate. I turned on my heel: I had someone.

Tucked beneath the roof, the music room retained the animal heat of the hundred girls who had practiced there hour after hour. I went inside. I flopped down at a desk. I could hear the sound of water dripping into a basin, I listened for each drop to fall. She did not know where I was, loving her. I wanted her to come up here because I could not imagine she would not foresee this. Twenty to twelve . . . I counted to six between two drops of water. Her step.

She was trampling on my heart, my belly, my forehead even before she came in. A city of light was coming toward me. This must be some devastating enchantment. I guessed that she was looking for me through the glass while I had been picturing her in the darkness beneath my eyelids. I did not look up, I did not emerge from the folds of my widow's weeds. Crows scattered, frost whitened the hazels. She was coming, she was breathing through my lungs.

"I've looked everywhere for you," said Isabelle.

Isabelle appeared behind me, she sobbed with happiness. She sat down on the bench.

We loved and we were holding each other: we held each other balancing on a wild rose petal. She considered my lips, she touched them with one rough hand:

"Is it you, really you?"

The hand was seeking truths on my eyelids.

Her face dropped, her face descended lower than my breasts.

"Your face is too far away," I said.

"I've torn your dress," said Isabelle.

She fixed my dress with a pin, she carried out her repairs while I breathed in the perfume of memories in her hair.

"Someone's coming!"

We sprang apart, we each ran to hide in

a different corner. An accompanist turned the key to her room. She passed by, drew away again, peaceful and statuesque.

"The monitor told me to take you to the doctor at four o'clock," said Isabelle.

I ran into her arms as she ran to mine.

"Quarter to twelve!" said Isabelle. "Come on, come on . . ."

We fell together on the steps to the stage.

"Quarter to twelve, Thérèse!"

I hesitated, for my fingers were stained with ink.

"Don't stop me!" I said, out of nervousness.

I was afraid of demeaning her by lifting up her skirt.

"Almost ten to twelve, Isabelle!"

"If you don't speak more softly we'll be caught," said Isabelle.

I lifted up her skirt; Isabelle shivered against my temple.

I ventured beneath the crumpled skirt: her underpants frightened me. She was quite indecent beneath her dress. My hand advanced between skin and jersey.

"Let me do it. Don't look if it shocks you," said Isabelle.

I looked.

She lifted herself up, she released my hand.

"Such impossible underpants," she said.

The hand of one entranced tugged them off, stuffed the garment into the pocket of her smock. Isabelle revealed herself there on the steps.

"They were gripping you tightly, my golden lamb. You're all rumpled. You feel my cheek there on you, my darling Mongolian. I'm combing you, untangling you, teasing you, my little brazier . . . You're glowing Isabelle, you're glowing . . ."

I stood up, I glared at her.

"Come back . . . Don't leave me."

"Are you sure?"

I was sadistic. Waiting and making her wait is a delicious perdition.

"What if someone discovers us," I dreamed aloud.

"I can't wait any longer," whimpered Isabelle. Her hands were clutching at her face.

I fell to my knees before the medallion, I gazed rapt at the shining in her tangle. I ventured in like a smuggler, my face first. Isabelle gripped me between scissoring legs.

"I'm looking; I'm caught," I said.

We waited.

Sex was filling our minds. Isabelle was split from head to toe. An incalculable number of hearts were beating in her belly, against my head.

"Yes, yes . . . slower. I said slower . . . higher. No . . . lower down. Almost . . . almost there . . . Yes . . . yes . . . That's almost it . . . Faster, faster, faster," she said.

My tongue was searching in the salty darkness, in the sticky darkness, over fragile flesh. The more I labored, the more mysterious became my efforts. I hesitated around the pearl.

"Don't stop. I tell you that's it."

I was losing it, regaining it.

"Yes, yes," moaned Isabelle. "You're there, you're there," she cried in ecstasy. "Go on. Please . . . there . . . yes, there . . . just there . . ."

Her anguish, her mastery, her orders, her contradictions were confusing me.

"You don't want to guide me," I said, alone outside our universe of fantasy.

I spoke to her between the lips of her sex.

"I'm doing nothing else," she said. "You're not thinking about what you're doing."

"I'm thinking too much," I said.

Tears of my sweat are soaking her pubic hair.

"Teach me . . . teach me . . ."

"Lift your face, look."

Lying on the steps of the stage, Isabelle sought within herself, found it.

"Come closer, look, look. That's it. If you lose it, you'll find it again. Oh, oh . . . No. Not now. You! You!"

I looked through her fingers' angle at her gilded hair, I shivered with the shivering of the muscles in her hand. The finger was twisting. Soon I would spew out the delights of her orgasm.

Her neck tensed, her mind was elsewhere. Her eyes opened: Isabelle was staring at paradise.

"You. Not me," she said.

She withdrew from herself, clenched her fist.

"A minute past twelve! They're in the refectory. Past twelve . . . I'm afraid I might be wrong."

"Yes, yes . . . Go on until tonight if we have to," she said.

I labored so hard that I tasted the flesh of fantasy. Too near her sex I thought that

I wanted to give her what she desired. My mind was caught up in flesh, my abnegation growing. When I lacked saliva I would make it. I did not know if it was mediocre or indeed wonderful for her, but when the pearl slipped away I would find it again.

"It will be there, it will always be there," said Isabelle.

Nostalgia and bliss were mixing together.

"That's it," she said.

She fell silent, she kept watch over her sensations.

I received what she was receiving, I was Isabelle. My effort, my sweat, my rhythm were exciting me. The pearl wanted what I wanted. I was discovering the little virile sex that we have. A eunuch was gathering courage.

"I'm going to come my love. So good: I'm going to come. It's too good. Keep going. Don't stop, don't stop. Forever, forever, forever . . ."

I sat up; I wanted to see a prophesy on our bellies.

"Don't let me go, don't leave me here," cried Isabelle panicking.

"Tell me when, won't you," I said, my face in the furnace of her sex.

"Yes, but don't leave me."

I persevered, nothing but a reflection of her.

"It's started. It's starting. It's rising. Through my legs, through my legs . . . Yes, my love, yes. Forever . . . go on . . . In my knees, in my knees . . ."

She was observing the sensation, she was seeking relief.

"It's rising, it's rising higher."

She fell silent. I was submerged and swept away with her. There were stigmata in my guts.

We thanked each other with fragile smiles.

"This time someone is coming. Hide. I'll go out, I'll stand in front of the window. Go to the dormitory . . . We'll leave together at four o'clock," Isabelle whispered.

"Your hair! Your hair!"

She tied the chaos and madness up in that twist; she walked out mistress of herself.

A girl ran up, along the corridor. I listened behind the door.

"You're out of your mind," Renée was saying. "You know what the time is? Twenty-five past twelve. I've looked for you everywhere: in the classrooms, in the study room, in the infirmary. The head is furious."

"Does she know?" Isabelle asked.

"She came into the refectory. She was horrified by your empty seat. But what were you doing?"

"I was in the chemistry lab. I was working. I must explain it to the head," said Isabelle.

"Thérèse has also disappeared. We thought she was sick in the dormitory. I took her lunch up to her. Nobody there. You're unbelievable," said Renée.

They went off.

The tray was there in my cell, with its cold leavings of meat, lentils, two small green apples.

Eat. Eat to be strong at four in the afternoon, I exhorted myself before swallowing down the miserable, tepid items of food.

"Are you quite better now?" asked a monitor whom I jostled with my tray at the bottom of the stairs.

"I'm going to the doctor at four," I said smugly. I ran into the playground to see her again.

"Isabelle is in trouble, Isabelle is working," Renée told me.

"In the future you will ask my permission to go up to the dormitory even if you are not feeling well," the new monitor said to me.

The girls were lining up to go in and study.

We all heard the chiming of the tram's little bell, the tracks' complaining as the tram drew away. The town's noises and effluvia were no longer my escape: school had become our trysting place, school was now my bracelet and my necklace.

Isabelle was studying. I opened a book, I heard:

"Faster, slower, go on, go on, it's started, it's starting, higher, lower, don't leave me, don't let me go, forever, forever . . . I'm going to come. It's so good. I'm coming. It's too good . . . Forever, forever . . . It's there, will always be there."

I listened to her voice until the end of study period.

"Twelve roses! What were you thinking?" I said to the day student. "I said two, not twelve. And a shoebox too. I'm in a fix now!"

"I hardly had any lunch thanks to you. I had to look for the box in the attic. It's all I could find to hide them in and you're still not happy! Just two roses looked mean. You can pay me when you've the money."

"I'll pay you right now but you'll have to keep them in your room. You've got to take them off my hands. I'll take two and you can give the others to your father and mother . . ."

"It was for a monitor!"

"No . . . but you've given me an idea."

"We can decide this later. I like big bouquets," the day student said.

She ran off and I ran off too, to the dormitory with the flowers.

"What are you doing here?" inquired the new monitor. "You're not permanently unwell!"

The fragrance of cheap shampoo smothered my roses when she looked out of her curtains.

"I was looking for you. I wanted to give you these flowers . . ."

"Where are they from?"

"I disobeyed you. A girl bought them for me. They are from a florist."

"We'll overlook it this time but don't do it again."

She was in raptures.

"I oughtn't dare," she said, "really, I ought not. Come in. Let's see what it is you're presenting to me."

Everywhere were doilies, cambrics, lawns, contrasting lights, ribbons, embroidered cushions that exuded femininity. She cut the string around the box with embroidery scissors. She pulled away the paper; her long hands were greedy.

"Roses . . ."

I leant over my flowers, my sacrifice that she dared not awaken.

"It's too much. I ought to scold you. Really, it's too much."

Fruitcake! I thought to myself. She clasped my hand in thanks.

I slept as usual, I regained energy, I was

refreshed, sitting at the back through the rest of my classes.

At four o'clock, Isabelle was waiting for me at the classroom door.

"I'm taking you to the doctor," she said.

"We were all right here," I said, beneath the general clatter.

"It's an order," said Isabelle. "I'm going up to the dorm to dress and it would be best for you to come up too."

Our connection was unravelling, the strength drained from my heart. To be going outside with her, this was incredible.

It was there that I rediscovered her.

Isabelle had left her cell, her hair loose, her shoulders wrapped in her Arab riding shawl; Isabelle was reassuring me with the costume of our first encounter. She was stroking the handle of her hairbrush.

"Let's go. Think of it: we're leaving," she said.

"Don't go back into your cell. So I never lose sight of you," I said.

The hand holding the brush fell back. The hair was snuffed out.

I ran to her:

"Go back to yours, be beautiful without me there to see it," I said.

Isabelle threw her brush into the passage. She was putting her shawl around my neck.

"I want to strangle you. I do want to," she said.

But she didn't pull it tight.

This intimacy in the passage disoriented me. I led her by the hand, I showed her the bouquet of roses:

"I gave them to her at half past one. You're not cross?"

"Cross! They're just flowers," she said, without looking back at them.

The shawl around her shoulders billowed with every step, her hair moved me more than the roses. I went back into my box:

"This appointment is a torment to me."

"Not me. I feel like walking out with you and that's what we'll do. We'll say that the doctor was called away for an emergency. I'll fix it."

Isabelle came back. She lifted my curtain.

"You aren't getting ready? Do you want me to help?"

"I'm not used to this. I'm a little scared."

She seized my wrists:

"Scared! Can't you see that I'm ready to sacrifice everything?"

"Even your studies?"

"My studies more than anything, as that would be the hardest thing," Isabelle said.

"I would not want that. I'd never want that," I said.

We got ready. The shouts from the playground were no longer our concern.

"I'm entrusting her to you," the head monitor said to Isabelle. "You have the letter with the number and the street name. You will find him there. He's expecting you. Come back with good news, won't you."

— 140 —

"Will you permit us a short stroll in town?" Isabelle asked.

"On condition that you don't take advantage. Don't run away," she called.

We had crossed the great courtyard calmly but the flowers, the lawn, the trees had all flown by. The concierge nodded to us.

We walked along the school wall, we heard a piano teacher's voice, his beating time with the ebony ruler that was always kept by the upright piano.

"Aren't you happy?"

"We were fine at school."

We had walked along one wall of Saint Nicholas's: the priests were teaching, the boys going wild.

"Can we go arm in arm?"

"We ought to keep from doing that," said Isabelle.

Just as we used to listen for them in the playground, the sounds of the tram and its bell rose up toward school. Soon the girls would hear the hum of the slow local service. Sleepy houses began to give way to shops; the squeal of the tram on its rails lingered out beyond school: we were in town.

Isabelle stopped in front of a display of leatherware. She wanted me to pause with her at this graveyard of black suede things:

"Do you like this stuff?"

"I like, I like . . . You know what I like," said Isabelle.

I was proud to feel as if we were two against the town.

"Will you ever forget me? I never will," said Isabelle. She was gazing at a paste buckle.

"You will always be alive in me. You will die with me," I said.

My eyes were closed, I imagined that she was speaking softly to me in the dormitory at night.

I slipped my arm under hers, I molded her gloved hand, I pushed my finger into the lozenge, as far as the hand's hollow. The idle shop assistant was watching us.

"The headmistress would say that we are comporting ourselves badly. Yes, give me your arm," said Isabelle.

We walked on, we skipped over the light beyond a church tower. The gentle tone of an ambulance sounded through our exaltation, the rattle of milk churns striking against each other, the driver snoozing at his wheel made me nostalgic for pools of buttercups.

We were running to outrun liberty, we were running alongside the depot's pinnacles of anthracite; we zigzagged in among the blue glittering, straightened out again near the stacked wedges. I remember the charcoal burner with the stoven-in face whom we puzzled, who vanished inside the depot, I remember his white eyes and the trolley he was pushing with his fingertips.

"What shall we do now?" inquired Isabelle.

"I don't know."

"I know," she said.

"Shall we take a walk? Shall we go to the waiting room? Pick up a railway platform ticket? Have tea in a patisserie?"

She brushed all this away with one hand.

"I know a place," said Isabelle.

". . ."

"Say something. I know a place for us to go together. Aren't you pleased?"

We were trotting along beside the stony wall of a factory. Somewhere, a while away, a beam thudded to the ground.

"Let's go to this hotel," said Isabelle. "Not exactly a hotel. A house."

I unlinked my arm from hers.

"You don't want to?"

"I don't know what it is."

"It's a house where a lady will receive us, a pleasant lady."

"How do you know that?"

"It's her business. She will have to be pleasant," said Isabelle.

We reached a square with an arc of trees pollarded down to stumps.

"Will you decide?"

"I'm afraid to," I said.

We marched furiously around the amputated trees.

"So? A yes or a no?"

"We were fine at school . . ."

"This will be far better than at school," said Isabelle.

I took her handbag, I carried it alongside my purse, I linked my arm in hers: twining together, our fingers made love.

"Aren't you hungry? There are some patisseries," I said, with a faint hope of distracting her from her plan.

"I've not been hungry since I met you. There it is. That's the one."

"Algazine, Dresses and Coats: is that the place?"

"Ring the bell, go on then, ring it. It's on your side."

"I couldn't bring myself to do it."

"Allow me," said a bearded man, "you'll allow me, since I take it you've not yet rung . . . Were that the case, however . . ."

"Consider it done," replied Isabelle.

The man raised the felt hat already in his hand; the door opened by itself.

"Ladies first," said the man.

He stepped aside, his hat still raised. Isabelle gave me a push. I went in first. Perished raincoats hanging from the coat stand there had seen their last rainfall long ago and, below them, gold-topped walking sticks with animal heads carved in wood and silver sheared off on every side like stems in a spray of flowers. The bearded man was wiping his shoes.

"You know your way, of course," he hinted, in a sybaritic voice quite unlike the way he had spoken outside.

"No!" said Isabelle.

We were standing against the wall, we had the damp of it at our backs while he was trotting about the corridor, hat in hand, briefcase under one arm. He crooked a forefinger, hesitated, then knocked twice on a glass door camouflaged by imitation stained glass.

"But, come in, do come in . . ."

The voice emanated from a mountain of goodwill.

He stroked his beard, opened the door.

"I pray you . . ."

He was staring at Isabelle's high-necked blouse.

I was expecting more dressmaker's mannequins, offcuts of fabric, reels of thread, where instead there were only plants, miniature shrubs, birds, cages.

"I'll go and look for her," the man said.

He vanished into a small courtyard that was pleasantly crowded with bulb geraniums, ivies, potted vines, ferns, watering cans, and shelves for the plants.

"Let's get out!" I said.

"Wait for her," said Isabelle sharply.

Isabelle was looking at a painting that had orange rocks and waves of blue jam. The birds singing in their cages were making the light sparkle.

"I pray you, please don't stand up for me," said the lady. "You must excuse me. I was tending to my duchesses."

She pointed at the plants with a rope of pearls that hung down to her stomach.

"You mustn't be noisy when we have company," she told the birds.

The man with his briefcase and the hat in his hand nodded to us: he left just as he had come.

"He couldn't find Mademoiselle Paulette. He apologizes," said the woman, her expression no less coarse.

Despite her great size, her age, her weight, she sprang over to perch on the table.

"I'm at your disposal."

Isabelle stood up.

"We have come for a room."

Mme Algazine contemplated us and played with her pearl necklace.

"We should like to hire one for about an hour," Isabelle said.

A cage suspended from a ring swung to and fro, the bird inside giving little peeps beneath its china cupola.

"I see," said Mme Algazine.

She tossed her pearls behind her, so they hung down her back.

"You are minors," she said.

She pranced off into the courtyard. Isabelle ground her teeth. But she was coming back with a tender lettuce leaf, which she poked between the bars of the swinging cage. She headed back into the courtyard just as buoyantly.

I stood up, I called:

"Madame!"

"Right away, my little ones, right away," she said condescendingly.

"Madame!" said Isabelle resolutely.

She reappeared once more.

"We should like to hire a room, I tell you."

Mme Algazine opened her eyes wide:

"Why did you not say so when you came in, my little kittens?"

"We did say it."

Sometimes the bright wings were battered against the cage bars; the wound in our minds was gray.

"You are minors . . . ? Obviously."

"Yes," we replied together.

"Are you boarders at the school . . . ? You are wearing the uniform."

"We will pay you, we have the money," said Isabelle.

"You'll pay afterward," said Mme Algazine.

Isabelle unbuttoned her cardigan but I put myself in front of her. Mme Algazine would see nothing of any chest beyond what was shielding it.

"Will you take a drop of port, will you want to eat a few teacakes in the room?"

"We will drink and eat whatever you like," said Isabelle. "Show us the way."

"Not shy are we . . . ?"

Mme Algazine opened the glass door, she pointed to the stairs with her necklace, which she handled as one would a hosepipe.

"Electricity is expensive, gas too, oil too, and matches too. Everything is expensive," said Mme Algazine, in the voice of her true nature.

The staircase was dark. On the landing we passed decrepit rooms, folding beds that had burst open, we bumped into boxes of crockery, drifts of fallen plaster, ragged curtains. Mme Algazine showed us the way, her eyes sliding distractedly over everything.

"Yours will be the first door," she said.

"Thank you, oh thank you," said Isabelle.

"I'll bring your port up to you shortly."

Mme Algazine retreated, alone and old, down the sordid staircase.

Isabelle took the key from the keyhole, she went in first.

"Two beds!" she said.

She wanted to close the door but she could not quite manage. The key she threw at the mantelpiece, where it fell to the floor. She flung her boarder's straw hat to the back of the room, pushed the table against the door.

"Take it off," she said, reproachfully, "we aren't paying anyone a visit here."

She sent my hat flying at the mirrored wardrobe, she undid my hair.

"Lie down with me on the tiles," she said.

My mouth met her mouth as a dead leaf meets the earth. We sank into that long kiss, we recited our wordless litanies, we were greedy, we smeared our faces with the saliva passed between us, we stared without recognizing each other.

"Someone's moving in the room next door," I said.

She sat up. I tortured her when I made her wait.

"Me, Isabelle. Not you."

I ravaged her as if she were struggling against me.

"Someone is moving in the room next door. Look, Isabelle, look, in the wall."

"It's a spyhole," she said.

"They can see us. I'm sure they can see us."

I lay down over her, I hid her from the strangers.

"Which 'they'?" asked Isabelle silkily.

"I don't know. The people in the room. Listen! The sound our bedsprings make in the dorm."

Isabelle stared. I had surprised her.

"Forget other people and lie down better than that," Isabelle said.

She scratched me, or perhaps she scraped her nails on the tiles.

"Our bedsprings at night . . . I'm begging you: listen."

Someone knocked.

"Open it," she said. "It's the door."

Someone tried to push the door open, they were speaking:

"What have you done here? Have you barricaded yourselves inside?"

I picked up the key, I pulled away the table. Mme Algazine pushed her head through the opening:

"You can take the tray from the landing yourselves, since you've locked yourselves in."

Lying on the floor in the middle of the room, Isabelle crossed her arms over her face.

I fetched the tray, I heard the groans of the bedsprings in the room next door. I came back into our room:

"Don't you want to drink it? You won't get up?"

"I want you to come here," said Isabelle.

"The sound our bed makes at night . . ."

"It isn't the sound of our bed at night," said Isabelle.

I listened. The regular rhythm was not like our fitful rhythm in Isabelle's box.

"Who is it?"

"A couple."

The bed went quiet. I was still listening.

"Come here," said Isabelle, "come here you, still in your clothes."

I came: my chest was burning through her dress.

"Marry me, marry me all over," moaned Isabelle. Her smile grew broader and I possessed her everywhere that skin met fabric: my arms, my legs were winding around her. I hid in her neck:

"The sound has started again."

I could not tear myself away from that regular cadence.

"Listen!"

"I can't hear anything," said Isabelle.

I was trapped by the rhythm, condemned to follow it, to hope for it, fear it, to edge closer to it.

"Let's drink the port," said Isabelle.

I was listening hard.

"Drink!" ordered Isabelle.

I obeyed. The amber heat filled my chest.

"Listen! Someone's screaming."

Isabelle shrugged:

"I can't hear anything."

She strutted around the room. Someone was sighing, whimpering.

Isabelle reached over the folding bed: she was rummaging in her bag.

"Less noise. They're complaining," I said.

Someone was immured in the bedroom next to ours, someone who was trying to escape but couldn't find a way out.

Isabelle was filing her nails.

"Stop me from hearing it!" I said.

Isabelle went on filing her thumbnail.

The last wail pierced as high as the North Star. Isabelle's nail file gnawed into the silence.

Isabelle put her file back in her handbag.

"We're wasting our time. Why did we rent this room?"

"I don't know anymore," I said.

Isabelle slapped me.

"I don't know, I don't know . . ."

Isabelle slapped me again.

"It's a couple. There's a couple in the next room," I said.

She took up the little coffee table, she threw it into the marble fireplace. Isabelle's fury bewitched me.

"Undress me," said Isabelle.

I took off her clothes, I laid them out one by one on the folding bed.

She was naked, severe, standing very straight in the center of the room. I took her hand, I led her over and with the other hand, as we passed, I righted the little table.

I fell on Isabelle, I laid bare the shape of her legs, of her instep; I saw myself in the mirror. The room was old; the mirror reflected back the buttocks and embraces of every couple. I took her leg in my arms, skimmed over it with my chin, my cheek, my lips. I stroked her back and forth as if with a bow; the mirror showed everything I did; the slaps she had given me tingled.

"You're slipping away from me," she said.

I looked in the mirror at her hands clasped over her pubic hair, I felt the pleasure of one alone.

"You won't undress, like me?" said Isabelle.

I was kissing her knee, looking at myself in the mirror, loving my gaze upon myself.

"You're neglecting me," said Isabelle.

I tore myself from the mirror: sex of such sweet depths. But the mirror attracted me, the mirror was summoning me back for more solitary embraces. I stroked Isabelle's lips and pubic hair with her finger. I held the pressure of our pleasure between my thighs.

"What are you doing?"

"Sleep a moment."

"I'm wondering if you love me," said Isabelle.

"I didn't feel like answering yes."

Isabelle sat up on the pillow, she crossed her legs. The gathered shapes of her were daunting.

"Look up. Such a fuss about nothing," said Isabelle.

A door opened, closed again.

"It's the couple!"

Isabelle stifled a yawn:

"Yes, a couple."

She opened her thighs:

"Say if you don't want to."

I threw myself at her sex. I would have preferred it to be simpler. I almost wanted to sew it back up all round.

"My darling trout, my beloved submarine pout. I'm coming back to you. I'm here. The couple has gone . . . We are alone . . . It's the pink brute. I love it, it devours me. I adore it without illusions."

"You're biting me, hurting me," said Isabelle.

"I admit it, my delicate, I admit it, my little burning flower."

"Yes . . . like in the music room, like in the music room . . . Gently . . . gently . . . That's almost right. Almost, almost . . ."

"You're talking too much, Isabelle."

I plunged my face back inside the holy image. I was licking, gulping, I stopped to rest but my rest was a mistake.

"Is that it?"

"That's it."

I went back to work: I had a sun to light up. I saw what she was seeing and what she was listening to with the sight and hearing of our sex, I anticipated everything she was anticipating.

"Still . . . still . . ."

A cat was licking, a cat was blindly toiling and stroking away.

"Long, so long," Isabelle intoned.

I was pressing on like a scratched record

circling round and round. Her pleasure was beginning in me. I came away for some air.

"They're listening to us, Isabelle!"

She closed her legs, seized up.

"Open the door, check," said Isabelle.

I waited, crouching there in my clothes.

"Open the door, come back quickly. I'm waiting for you," said Isabelle.

"The door is too far. You want me to start all over again!"

I became my most winning, I seduced the inmost folds with my finger's singing, I stroked the sex as I watched it in the mirror. I looked on. I could see the mist of someone breathing under the door and I could see it in the mirror too.

"Come and lie down with me," said Isabelle.

"There's someone there. I saw them."

"You're torturing me!" said Isabelle.

I threw her jacket over her, pulled away the table and stepped outside. The brooding staircase.

"There's no one there," I said.

"Don't touch me again," said Isabelle.

Isabelle lay down on her front.

I stayed standing next to the bed. I couldn't decide whether to undress.

"I ought to strangle you," said Isabelle.

She rolled over onto her back:

"Shall we go? Shall I get dressed?"

"Don't deny me your hair. Not a bun."

"I'm redoing my hair. You're abandoning me," said Isabelle.

"Oh, what have I done! There was someone there. I wasn't dreaming it," I said.

"You were raving."

I let myself drop onto the bed:

"Don't stop me . . . Take your hands away, forgive me. I will love you. You will teach me. Yes, I'm coming. You are beautiful. Your legs are beautiful too. I do want to. Take my finger. I'll give and receive, give and receive."

I abandoned her again. I ran around the

room, I brought her clothes, which I threw at her and at her streak of saliva.

"You are infernal. I shall end up cursing you," said Isabelle, suddenly strained.

"People can see us, they are looking at us," I complained.

"Where?"

Isabelle rolled back onto her chest: she was shaking the bars on the bed.

"There's an eye. I can see it."

"Be quiet, be quiet! Nearly . . . nearly . . . It's growing, it's growing," Isabelle said.

She turned onto her back, she bent her legs and brought them right up to the dip of her stomach. She was consuming herself.

"It's my fault if you don't get anywhere," I said.

"I won't get anywhere and it is your fault," said Isabelle.

"In the window . . . the eye . . ."

Isabelle stood up, walked naked and dignified across the room.

"It's hunger, it's exhaustion, my poor Thérèse. I can't see a thing. There is nothing but dust and spiderwebs in that window."

Isabelle got back into bed, she stretched out under the American eiderdown.

"You really don't want to get undressed? It's warm under here," she said.

She wiggled her foot, she was provoking me beneath that satin!

"It's nice here . . . Why are you standing around?"

"I'm afraid of the eye."

"So come here, then!"

Reaching out from the bed, she took my hand.

"Let's go, Isabelle. Let's escape from this house. I'll help you to dress on the landing," I said tenderly.

She let go of my hand.

"A moment ago you were afraid of the landing."

"Now it's the window," I said.

She shrugged.

"You're afraid of everything."

"I saw that eye."

Isabelle was laughing.

"Don't you want us to go really?" I said.

She turned away from me.

I ran out onto the landing and she came to join me but she came naked. Her mound was pronounced. There could be a kind of personality in that, too.

"I'm cold because of you," said Isabelle.

She was dragging me back by my hands.

"We'll do it together," she said, in a voice that was meant to be encouraging.

"I'm frightened of the room."

"Together . . . at the same time . . . We will call out as much as we like. We'll scream together."

We went back into the bedroom.

"I would prefer to go."

"That would be preferable," said Isabelle.

She was getting dressed. Again I ran onto the landing, I left her to the intimacy of her suspender belt, to her regret. But every atom of that house was a spy.

"Your handkerchief, your hat . . . Where are you, little scaredy-cat?"

She came to look for me on the landing.

Her hand swept over my hair, the mauve scent of her powder shivered my arms and legs into pieces.

She held out her hand, for me to lean on and get back on my feet. We kissed.

"Let's look once more," said Isabelle.

Abandoned, the place had reassumed an air of innocence.

We felt our way down through the darkness of the staircase; we managed not to crush the little, fluttering wings of our reconciliation, we took the spring back to its source.

"You had a room with two beds . . . Is that correct?"

"A folding bed and a double," said Isabelle.

"Have you any money?"

Isabelle held out her money and I held out mine.

"Which should I take?"

"Both."

"Yes, both," said Isabelle.

"Did you find it a good bed?"

Mme Algazine looked at us. She was counting the notes.

"Yes," I said dully, "it was good." Isabelle gave her hat a punch.

"No. Your beds are not good," said Isabelle.

Mme Algazine scratched her chin with our folded notes.

"We are in a hurry. Please, open the door," said Isabelle.

Mme Algazine went on tickling her chin with the notes.

"Was the port not good?"

"Excellent but we must be going," said Isabelle.

"The door is open," said Mme Algazine, by way of farewell.

"We still have half an hour left to buy things. We mustn't dally," said Isabelle.

"What things?"

"You'll see," said Isabelle.

Her gloved hand seized mine.

"Give me your bag . . . so I can carry it."

"You like that, carrying my bag?" she asked.

The evening light at six o'clock was not crisp; the houses were growing bored.

I plucked a betrothal flower out of a clump of privet, in the street with the charcoal depot, I stuck it in Isabelle's fist.

". . . I was counting the nights we'll have until the summer holidays. We'll have plenty," said Isabelle.

She led me into the best tearoom in town.

The tables were not yet cleared away, the ring of chatter lingered, the scent of blond tobacco mixed with the scents of the departed customers.

"Why are we here? Are you hungry?"

"No," said Isabelle.

"Me neither."

"Give me my bag, though," said Isabelle.

I gave it to her and fled from the patisserie.

At last I bought the two roses I had wanted for her. I saw her again while I was at the till, paying for the flowers. Isabelle was looking for me, biting her lip. My love was clear eyed but it was love. I hid the flowers inside my jacket.

"Very clever!" she said. "Why did you run out?"

We were going back up the rue de la Maroquinerie.

"Let's stop here. Choose the bag you like best and I'll buy it for you. I will carry it when we're alone in the corridors at school," I said.

"It's as if you were giving me a keepsake, as if you were going away. Don't buy me anything," said Isabelle.

The shop assistant was setting a box calf drum in a corner of the shop window.

"Let's go back to school. It's time to go," said Isabelle.

"I would but you're not moving."

"I'm frightened of the future," said Isabelle.

"Frightened . . . you!"

"I'm miserable, Thérèse."

The town snapped in two.

"If you're unhappy I will die."

"Don't talk. Hold my arm tight, look at the window display. We must go back to school but I feel as though we mustn't. I'm frightened," Isabelle said again.

"Let's leave school. We won't die of hunger."

"They'll catch us. We would be parted straight away. Keep me warm," said Isabelle.

"Don't be unhappy."

"Look! In the mirror. See . . . they're pointing at us," said Isabelle.

It was raining threatening fingers. Still,

our confidence was enough to charm the cobbles. The azure sky between far-off branches mussed our hair.

"Are we running away?"

"Where to?" said Isabelle.

"To Madame Algazine's."

"That was a bad idea."

Our school reappeared; we felt our connection to the great, nameless family that would be studying in the study rooms before dinner. I went by the dormitory for the sake of the roses, and hid them in my dirty laundry bag.

At seven o'clock, Isabelle came into the refectory following the others.

I threw my napkin under the table, I bent down to whisper that I would carry her handbag and that I would carry the zephyr too, if the zephyr were tiring her.

She was coming. I counted her steps down the long passage. Fifteen drumrolls thundered in my heart. How many times was I put to death during her coming. The same citadel of love was nearing: my throat contorted.

Isabelle was watching the ardent blue: Isabelle loved me at the hour of sunset on the stained-glass window. The monitor called my name from the far end of the refectory.

"Do wake up," said another girl.

Isabelle was also calling me; Isabelle was sucking the colors from me:

"Do you love me? Do you still love me?" I entreated with every look.

The monitor told me that I should not go to study, that I should go up to the dormitory to rest, that it was an order from the head monitor.

The day was declining, my cell fading away, down blowing from the lips of my absent beloved. Night was taking over; night, our swans' wing covering. Night, our canopy of gulls.

I focused my flashlight, shone it on the flowers I had bought, savored the air of occasion. The night drew outlines around the roses in the gardens outside.

I began the leisurely toilette of a bride-to-be; as I soaped, I hid fronds of orange flowers between my legs, under my arms; I paraded a trail of cool scent around my cell; I proceeded into the passage with the scepter of our future, I entered Isabelle's cell: her belongings were austere, her bed abandoned. I slipped out of time. I stayed waiting, my face hidden in my hands.

The girls came in like an invading army; the monitor had turned on the lights. I could not escape. The girls were running down the passage, shouting, laughing.

"You! In my box!"

Arm outstretched, she was clutching the curtain that she had roughly wrenched back on its rail, into this frame she brought her hair wild at the close of the day, her haunted face, her potent eyes.

My dressing-gown cord fell onto the rug. Isabelle stared at my nightgown.

"Oh," she said, "it's so white . . ."

She threw me onto her bed, she entered but drew out again straight away. A little girl had lifted the curtain, a little girl was looking at us. She fled, she screamed:

"Blood, I saw blood!"

"Back to your box!" ordered Isabelle.

Isabelle looked at her three bloody fingers.

I ran out.

"What is going on?" asked the monitor, leaving her bedroom and coming a few paces into the passage.

I slipped into my bed, I looked at the red stain on my nightgown.

"Just a cut. It's already dry," said Isabelle.

"A bad one?" asked the monitor.

There was a troubling silence.

"I bleed easily," said Isabelle.

I got out of bed, I repaired the damage inflicted by my warrior.

"Isabelle . . ."

Wresting her name from me, the new monitor tarnished my Isabelle.

"Yes," replied Isabelle, quite naturally, as she went on brushing her teeth.

"Is it really nothing, just a cut?" asked the monitor.

"It's nothing at all," said Isabelle, her mouth full of dental paste froth.

Girls were chattering over the vigorous fragrance of the eau de cologne; Isabelle was getting into bed and the bedsprings were free to creak.

The monitor began her round.

"Good night, mademoiselle," murmured one girl.

The lights were turned out in the passage.

A foolhardy lover brushed against my curtain, left a little of her secret in the curtain's folds. The whisperings sank into an abyss. The dormitory gave way to sleep.

I too was heavily struck with drowsiness.

I dreamed: Isabelle was holding my wrist, trailing my hand and the flowers over my sex. I woke up lacerated, greedy.

I waited by the window with the roses, imagining Isabelle's arrival. The curtain lifted just as I was gazing at it, seeing nothing. Isabelle came in; centuries of love sighed. Isabelle in a negligee, the broad-winged collar of her nightgown folding down over her dressing-gown lapels, Isabelle had the preoccupied gaze of a queen.

"Hello."

"Hello."

I laid the roses on the bed, I let myself slide down, I pressed kisses on her feet. Isabelle did wish me to adore her. The flowers fell, we feared that the leaves' rustling might awaken the monitor, but the night's surprise was Isabelle's face next to mine.

"You put on your schoolgirl dress," she said.

She felt the crispness of the pleats. Her

cheek followed the slope from my groin to my knee.

A water lily bloomed in my stomach, the veil of the white lady floated over my moors.

"Come," she said, with assurance.

We crossed the passage, we entered Isabelle's box.

The doily on her night table lent its impulse of whiteness, the pillow was innocent. She was breaking the flowers' stems in two.

Where had my roses come from? When had she taken the tooth-glass from the dressing table? When had she poured the water? When had she bent over the washbowl? I was considering Isabelle in the shadows of all the world's countries.

"Where are you?" she said.

I shook the night from my shoulders as you shake snow from a winter hood; the roses leaning over the lip of the tooth-glass were my equals, roses for a boarding-school girl.

"Breathe them in," said Isabelle.

I was struck dumb.

"Breathe them in!"

She put the glass and its roses in my hands, tossed her hair back, revealed her high, open collar to me, her neck. My flashlight and the tooth-glass knocked together.

I trailed garlands of bronze, suspended cast-iron roses around her neck.

"Ceremony, ceremony," I said, severely.

Isabelle was shielding her neck, inflamed all over by my touch. She stepped back but watched me intimately. The distress was growing; the sky, a single cloud, lingered inside me: the rope of my desire was spinning out between my legs. Eye to eye, we summoned each other. We had either to die or bring ourselves to act. I came to.

"Open your collar."

I had my eyes closed, I was listening

for the sound of her unbuttoning her nightgown.

"I'm waiting for you," said Isabelle.

The rosy eyes were looking at me, the rose in the tooth-glass was leaning their way. My arms fell back; I was ready to become their martyr. They were sending out their shafts of warmth and already their silken shapes were heavy against my empty hands. I moved toward them and, like fruit, they ripened without spoiling. They were swelling: I entrusted the sun to them. Leaning against the partition, Isabelle was watching them as I did.

"Do up your collar," I said.

As on other nights, a whisper from one of the girls refreshed the night.

Isabelle smiled down at her breasts. I know where I would make love to her if I had her still: I would make love to her in a sheepfold, among the low-slung ewes' bellies.

Isabelle undid my nightgown, Isabelle hesitated, Isabelle was greedy. I was not helping her: I was savoring the ardor of a queen let loose. The sigh tumbled from the tree of silence, two throats thrust forward, four springs of sweetness shone out. Breasts suckled my breasts, absinthe was flowing in my veins.

"Better than this," begged Isabelle.

It did not leave my mouth as we dropped slowly onto the parquet.

I was sheltering it in my hands, holding on to its weight of warmth, of pallor, of affection. My belly was starving for illumination.

"Caress it," said Isabelle.

"No!"

I opened my mouth, it entered. I was biting down on precious veins, I remembered that bruising: it was choking me. My hand faded away in smoke, my hand dropped, resonating. Such a crowd of voyeurs, the shadows above us . . . You're looking down.

"What can you be afraid of?" said Isabelle.

I was muttering evasively about her neck. Magnets below Isabelle's chin were attracting me. My flashlight fell onto the rug.

"You'll get us caught!" said Isabelle.

"Your neck . . ."

She accepted the worship without basking in it.

Sly, I looked for the channel between her breasts and it was in response to my hypocritical gaze that she drew the collar of her gown closed. The gateway between her eyes and mine opened: we had regained the freedom of loving and looking. My gaze was returned like waves that crash down into themselves. I tamed the mirrors in her eyes, she tamed the mirrors in my eyes.

Isabelle settled on my lap:

"Say that we have time. Say it."

I did not reply.

The night was cooling our coupled lips.

"I am counting the hours we have left," said Isabelle.

The time came and moved on with its veils of black crepe. I was sheltering Isabelle with her long hair, winding it around her neck.

"Stay, stay some more," said Isabelle.

We held each other close, but we could not be sheltered from the great tide of hours; rather, night in the great courtyard, night from the town came over us.

"I'm cold," said Isabelle.

We heard a tree's shroud cracking in the wind.

"I'm frightened of the time that's passing," said Isabelle.

I made myself laugh. I turned on the light.

Isabelle looked at her watch:

"It's eleven o'clock, Thérèse. Turn it off."

She stood up: my seasick knees took me aback.

I fell at her feet, reunited with my bouquet.

"You must come to my mouth," said Isabelle.

I heard the rustle of funereal skirts. It was her hair that she was pushing away.

Isabelle shook the battery inside her watchcase.

"I must put the clock forward," I said, "we must do that."

She gave me her wristwatch:

"What else have we left now?"

"We shall stay ahead," I said.

I was molding a spun-glass doe, touching it without quite reaching it, but with my jeweller's tongue I dropped jewels into her mouth.

She wiped her lips with my hand, she pretended indifference.

"Don't go on."

She escaped my arms: there I was, powerless over the swarms languishing in my belly. Isabelle threw herself at my neck.

I took her up where I had left her. Our mouths one on the other opened into an easy dream. I tipped her upside down without losing my hold, I cupped her head in my hands as I always did, as I would have held the weight of a decapitated head. I entered. I noticed a trace of dental paste, a souvenir of freshness. Our limbs were ripening, our cadavers decomposing. Exquisite decay. I half-opened my eyes: Isabelle was watching me. I had declared war inside her mouth; I had been beaten. An oriental melody snaked among my bones, the threnody circled in my elbows, in my knees. There was a blessing in my blood; my death gave way to corruption. I was purifying her gums, I still wanted to obliterate Isabelle with my kiss. I thanked her twice with two other, businesslike kisses on her hands. Little heads were turning: nighttime sparrows observing us.

We got into bed, we listened to the

sheets' crispness. The night was leaning in and watching over us, the night was offering us a virginal final scene.

Isabelle took my hand, she pressed it down on the gilded tangle.

"Don't move," said Isabelle.

My hand aspired to the moistness of a cowshed. Isabelle would come with her arm crossed over mine, with her forthright hand, with a dream that would come to rest on my hair.

"Be quiet, be quiet!"

Isabelle was speaking to the two hands, each cradling its kingdom.

Inside, my calves are full of rags; I bear the summer weight of the climbing rose. The hordes . . . have pity . . . now I can no longer hold you at bay.

I was watching, hoping for a movement from the delicate hand. My heart was beating in my eyelids, in my throat.

"I can't go on!"

I have destroyed everything: our hands, our arms, our tangled hair, the silence, the night.

We parted, we waited for each other, we saw fear's chasm open between us. If the thread of our waiting should break, we shall fall into the bowels of the earth. I lay facedown, I hugged myself close with my fever.

Isabelle dragged me into the middle of the bed, she mounted me, she lifted me up, let the air flow around my armpits.

You rode me: this wasn't new. You lit a powder keg of memories. Encountering you, I found a sense in my abyss.

Isabelle sawed at my shoulders, braced and bucked, scaled me, opened herself, drove deep, rocked from side to side and made me rock. The watchers revived, the octopus recommenced its struggle.

"Don't leave me anymore," I said.

Night, belly of silence.

Isabelle rose slowly, slowly, her inward

lips closing on my hip. Isabelle toppled.

I felt for her hand, I laid it on my back, I moved it down to below my waist, I put it down by my anus.

"Yes," said Isabelle.

I waited, I gathered myself.

"This is new," said Isabelle. Shy, it entered, Isabelle spoke:

"My finger is warm, my finger is happy."

The anxious finger did not dare.

We listened, we were ecstatic. The finger would always be importunate inside the greedy sheath. I contracted, to encourage it, I contracted, to imprison it.

"Further, I want further," whimpered Isabelle, her mouth squashed against my neck.

She pressed into the impossible. Again the knuckle, again the prison around it. We were at the mercy of the poor, diminutive finger.

The weight on my back meant that the finger was not giving up. The furious finger stabbed and stabbed. A maddened eel was dancing with death against my insides. My eyes were listening, my ears seeing: Isabelle was infecting me with her brutality. Let the finger right through the town, let it rupture the abattoirs. The burning was hurting me, our limitation hurt even more. But the dogged finger awakened my flesh; but the blows made me keener. My intoxication was layered in thick brushstrokes, in a warbling of spices, I opened myself up to the hips.

"The bed is shaking too much," said Isabelle.

The dilated flesh was grateful, severe pleasure spilled out among the petals. Sweat dripped from Isabelle's forehead onto my back.

"Don't move. So I can stay inside you," said Isabelle. We abided. I squeezed, in my turn.

"Oh yes!" gasped Isabelle.

I was sucking it in, driving it back, I

changed it into a dog's phallus, naked, red. It reached up to my esophagus. I was listening to Isabelle who was pressing lightly, who was following the growing tide, enjoying the outward ripples. The finger emerged from a cloud, vanished into another. My ardor claimed Isabelle, a crazy sun whirled in my flesh. Alone, Isabelle's body ascended the calvary of my back. I was suspended in my intoxication. My legs weakened in their paradise. Refreshed, my calves were ripening. I was softened to the point of ineffable decay, I was unendingly dissolving into happiness after happiness in my own ashes. Isabelle's finger slid out methodically and left pools of pleasure behind in my knees. It dropped me. Its going, slow ship of harmonies. We listened to the last of the cadence.

"You had nothing."

"Had nothing, I!" said Isabelle.

She laughed into my neck. The hilarity in her face was tropical.

"Had nothing!"

She pressed my hand between her lips, then my mouth dodged hers. We did not let these moments run together.

"Suffocate me," said Isabelle.

She lay back while I smothered her and while I labored to turn her into a beauty spot on my left breast. I was squeezing her, I was shivering like blades of grass in winter.

"Yes, you love me," said Isabelle.

I sat up, I had diamonds of frost on my shoulders.

I was remembering, I saw myself under the apple tree: my mother was taking me into a meadow for our own, intimate party, when the winter wind used to overthrow April, when the summer wind dulled November's edge. Twice a year we would settle down under the same apple tree, set out our picnic while the wind and its retinue of airs blew into our mouths and whistled in our hair. We would spread foie gras on crusty bread, drink champagne out of the same glasses as our beer, smoke a

Camel or two, watch the youthful quivering of the wheat in the blade, the aged shivers of the thatched roofs. A merry-go-round for gulls, the wind spun above our love and our picnic.

I wrapped Isabelle's name in velvet before pronouncing it, I listened in my head to the intonation of the sentence I would say to her.

"Won't you turn to me?" I asked.

Isabelle turned around. I threw myself into the Vale of Roses. The tiny lights in my skin desired the tiny lights in Isabelle's skin, the air grew thinner. We could do nothing without the meteors that would carry us in their wake, that would toss us one into the other. We were in thrall to irresistible forces. We dropped from consciousness but were still the unit of us against the night of the dormitory. Death dragged us back to life: we returned by many ports. I could see nothing, hear nothing, yet my senses were those of a visionary. We were entwined: a miracle was fading instead of shining forth.

"Together, together . . ."

She was stroking her chest with my hand:

"Lean in. Together, together . . . No, no . . . not right now."

She dropped back.

"Your hand, your hand," moaned Isabelle.

We worked from memory, as if we had embraced already in a world before our birth, as if we were reforging a link. Isabelle's hand against my hip, arousing me, was my own; my hand on Isabelle's side was hers. She was my reflection, I her reflection: two mirrors making love. Our joint excursion did not falter when she threw her hair back from her face, when I pushed back the sheets. I listened in her fingers to what my fingers were singing to her. We were learning, understanding that buttocks are responsive creatures. Our hands were so light that I could follow the down on Isabelle's skin curving against my arm, the curve of my down against hers. We explored down, we climbed back up the crevice between our clenched thighs with hidden fingernails, we were provoking, we were suppressing our quivering. Our skin was leading each hand and its double. We carried off the velveteen rains, the waves of muslin from crotch down to instep, we went back on ourselves, we were prolonging a rumbling of sweetness from our shoulders to our heels. We stopped.

"I'm waiting for you," said Isabelle.

Her flesh was flaunting pearls everywhere.

"I'll never find it," I said.

Her arm lifting beneath mine made my arm lift. Isabelle was examining her body. She replaced my hand; she began the motion with her hand on mine; she left me to my motion.

"Concentrate," said Isabelle.

The air was heavy, the air was barbaric.

I rocked it, sharpened it, released it from the folds of its decline, I gave it confidence. I would not recall it all like this had I not given it my soul and my life. The pearl made the finger keener and the finger became flesh of our flesh: the motion was also there in our heads. Flesh was polishing my finger and my finger polishing Isabelle's flesh. The motion was happening in spite of us: our fingers' dreaming. I loosened the departed, I was anointed through and through with pagan oils.

Isabelle sat up, she chewed at a lock of my hair:

"Together," she said.

Infiltrations of languor, fissures of delight, wetlands of trickery . . . The leaves of lilacs rolled out their sweetness, the spring began its death throes, the dust of the dead was dancing in my light.

I was at last myself while I was ceasing, at last, to be.

The visit to my paradise was near.

"Tell me when."

"I'll tell you."

I was leaving my skeleton behind, floating above my dust. At first the pleasure was rigid, difficult to bear. The sensation began in my foot, it flowed through flesh once more grown pure. We left our fingers in the old world, we burst open with light, we were flooded with bliss. Our limbs crushed with pleasure, our guts incandescent . . .

"It's rising, it's rising . . ."

"Never ending, never . . ."

The veil tickled the sole of my foot, the finger spun in white-hot sun, a velvet flame twisted in my legs. Come from far away, the veil flew off even further. Walking on waves . . . I know what this means for the torrent of my thighs. I had been brushed by the mantle of the madness that never rests, I had been crushed as much as caressed by a spasm of pleasure.

"Together."

"It was together . . ."

Rest, heavenly curfew. The same death in soul and body. Yes, but death with a zither, with a bullet in the head. Our silence: the periwinkle silence of maps of the night sky. Our stars beneath our eyelids: tiny crosses.

"Don't go quiet," said Isabelle.

"I'm not. I'm carrying you."

I was carrying the child most like her that she could give me: I was carrying the child of her presence.

She soothed my neck with her hair, with her cold little nose.

"Say something . . ."

"I can't. I have you here . . ." I guided her hand:

"I have you here and here . . ."

I led her hand over my belly.

"Crook your arm," she said, "crook it as if we were walking out together."

She gave me her arm and we strolled between Little Bear and Great Bear in our map of the stars.

My blood rushed toward her in jubilation. I turned the flashlight on.

Her pubic hair was not twinkling; it had grown thoughtful. I embalmed Isabelle with my lips, with my hands. Pale sleeping girls were breathing all around her; shades hungry for pallor whirled above her. I opened her lips and killed myself before looking. My face was touching it, my face moistening it. I began to make love to it out of plain friendship.

"Better than that."

I could not do more.

Isabelle thrust my face deep.

"You shall speak, you shall say it," she said.

There was a collision of clouds in my intestines. My brain was wild with greed.

"You are beautiful . . ."

I was picturing her. I was not lying.

Two petals were trying to swallow me. It was as if the eye of the flashlight saw better because it was the first to see.

"Speak," begged Isabelle, "I'm alone."

"You are beautiful . . . It's so strange . . . I don't dare to look anymore."

Its language all yawnings, the monster that made requests and gave answers was frightening me.

"Warm me again," I said.

The shadows' rustling at three in the morning made me shiver.

"Sleep a moment," she said, "I'll keep watch."

"Have I disappointed you?"

"That is for us to face squarely, like everything else."

The night would be gone, soon the night would leave us nothing but tears.

I focused the light; I was not afraid of my wide-open eyes.

"I can see the world. It is coming from you."

"Be quiet."

Dawn and her shrouds. Isabelle was

combing her hair in a zone by herself, where her hair was always loose.

"I don't want the daylight to come," said Isabelle.

It is coming, it will come. The day will shatter the night over an aqueduct.

"I'm afraid of being parted from you," said Isabelle.

A tear dropped into my garden at half past three in the morning.

I forbade myself the least thought so that she would be able to fall asleep inside my empty head. Day was taking over from the night, day was blotting out our weddings; Isabelle was falling asleep.

"Sleep," I said, near the hawthorns that had waited all night for the dawn.

I stole out of bed like a traitor; I went straight to the window. High in the sky there had been a battle, and the battle's heat was ebbing. The mists were beating a retreat; here and there, in isolated patches, night lingered, greying at the edges. Celestial dawn had come alone and no one would salute her.

"Are you going?" asked Isabelle.

"Sleep."

"Come back. My arm is cold."

"Listen . . . There's someone studying."

"What I used to do before I knew you," said Isabelle.

Already a bedlam of birds in one tree, already; first glimmerings already pecked away . . .

"I'll do what you want," I said.

I licked.

Kneeling on the pillow, Isabelle shook just as I was shaking. Let my flaming face, my mouth, be parted from her face, from her mouth. My sweat, my saliva, the lack of space, my situation as a slave in the galleys, condemned to ecstasy without respite since I fell in love with her: all bewitched me. I slaked my thirst with brine, I fed myself on hair.

I see the new day's half mourning, I see the tatters of the night, I smile at them. I smile to Isabelle and, forehead to forehead, I play at butting horns with her so as to forget what is dying. The melody of the bird that sings and hastens the morning's beauty exhausts us: perfection is not part of this world even when we come upon it here.

"The monitor is up!" said Isabelle.

The sound of the water in the basin ages us. She has gained strength while we have lost ours. The monitor was washing the residue of sleep from her skin.

"You'll have to go," said Isabelle.

To leave her like an outcast, to leave her in secret also saddened me. There were millstones weighing down my feet and I was learning the odor of our sweat by heart.

I sat down on her bed. Isabelle raised her desolate face to me:

"I don't want you to go. No, go on. It's too dangerous."

I loved Isabelle without show, without raptures: I offered her my life without a word.

Isabelle stood up, she took me in her arms:

"Will you come every evening?"

"Every evening."

"We'll never leave each other?"

"We'll never leave each other."

My mother took me back home.

I never saw Isabelle again.

A STORY OF CENSORSHIP

Here is *Thérèse et Isabelle* just as Violette Leduc originally wrote it, complete with those precious and acerbic pages that were unpublished until now, its bare and violent language demonstrating a liberty of tone such as no female writer in France had dared to adopt before Leduc.

Thérèse et Isabelle formed the first section of a novel, *Ravages,* which Leduc presented to the publisher Gallimard in 1954. Judged "scandalous," this work was censored by the publisher. Encouraged by Simone de Beauvoir, Leduc had begun writing it in spring of 1948. Two years earlier, she had published her début novel *L'Asphyxie* ("Asphyxia"), a fictional recreation of her childhood in a small town in Northern France, where she had lived with her mother's "blue, hard" eyes as well as with a loving grandmother. She was also then preparing a prose poem for publication, *L'Affamée* ("Starved Woman" or "Craving Woman"), which recounted her "impossible" passion for de Beauvoir. Two masterpieces that went unnoticed by the wider public but were greeted with enthusiasm by the literary elite of the time. Leduc was then what we call "a writer's writer."

Ravages was to be her first true novel, a project of protracted gestation that turned out to be riddled with problems, as Leduc's correspondence shows. While suffering from loneliness and from her infatuations with inaccessible people, Leduc revised and reconstructed her former passions on paper. "I have noted the gulf that stretches between the life I am leading and the eroticism of the book I'm writing," she confided to de Beauvoir.

In its original version, *Ravages* was intended to retrace the three love stories of its heroine Thérèse. These were inspired by, if not calqued on, the three liaisons that had marked Leduc's youth: a carnal coupling with a fellow schoolgirl; the time she spent living with a schoolmistress; and her encounter with a man whom she was to marry long afterward. This brief marriage ended with a suicide attempt by the author and an abortion that took her to death's door. Leduc was to devote three years to writing "Thérèse et Isabelle," the first part of her book. The challenge was considerable:

> I am trying to render as accurately as possible, as minutely as possible, the sensations felt in physical love. In this there is doubtless something that every woman can understand. I am not aiming for scandal but only to describe the woman's experience with precision. I hope this will not seem anymore scandalous than Madame Bloom's thoughts

at the end of Joyce's *Ulysses*. Every sincere psychological analysis, I believe, deserves to be heard.

Nevertheless, Leduc was assailed by doubts: "As for my work at the moment, I am discouraged," she admits to de Beauvoir. "I find myself thinking it a pointless book full of schoolgirls' follies I thought it was sexual narcissism, mere titivation." De Beauvoir was convinced that Leduc would succeed in evoking "feminine sexuality as no woman has ever done: with truth, with poetry, and more besides." Nevertheless, she was at a loss as to what to do with the audacity of Leduc's language: "There are some excellent pages; she knows how to write in bursts, but as for publishing this, impossible. It's a story of lesbian sexuality as crude as anything by Genet," she told Nelson Algren.

As revealed by her handwritten notebooks with their variants, their pages struck out or glued together, Leduc was aiming for a miniaturist's precision in her descriptions of the erotic scenes. In her role as primary reader, and in spite of their literary value, de Beauvoir advised her against keeping certain passages for she knew "exactly where one might go too far" with a publisher. She was not mistaken.

When, in 1954, de Beauvoir at last presented the manuscript of *Ravages*—already toned down in a meticulous "cleansing" process—to Raymond Queneau and Jacques Lemarchand, both members of Gallimard's reading committee, they were disconcerted. Although he appreciated the novel's qualities, Queneau judged the first section "impossible to publish openly," while Lemarchand wrote: "It's a book of which a fair third is enormously and specifically obscene—and which would call down the thunderbolts of the law. The book also includes a number of successful passages. The story about the schoolgirls could, in itself, constitute a rather beguiling tale—if the author would agree to draw a veil over some of her operational techniques. Published as it is, this book would become a scandal."

At a meeting with Leduc, Lemarchand proved unyielding. Despite de Beauvoir's support for the book, he declared that to publish the "story about the schoolgirls" it would be necessary to "take out the eroticism while keeping the emotions." He also demanded that several passages from the novel's second section be cut, notably the passage in the taxi about touching "the crumpled skin, fragile as an eyelid" of a penis. The description of the abortion (then illegal) with which the text ended would also be considerably censored. Lemarchand found it "too long, too technical;" Gallimard's legal adviser thought it like a "vindication of abortion."

"Hard day with Violette Leduc," de Beauvoir tells Sartre in May 1954. "She got out of bed where she had thrown herself with a fever of thirty-nine degrees following the meeting with Lemarchand. The doctor told her that that's what caused it. I made her have lunch in the Bois, take a walk to Bagatelle, and I did my best to console her. The taxi scene literally scandalizes people: Queneau, Lemarchand, Y Levy; I sense that they feel personally offended, being male."

This meeting broke Leduc as both writer and woman, by forcing her to give up on *Thérèse et Isabelle*, the best of her book, its most sincere and most daring part. It was her favorite piece out of all her own writing. They had "cut her tongue out." She experienced this censorship as a laceration, an amputation. Almost twenty years later, in *La Chasse à l'amour* ("The Hunt for Love"), a posthumous part of her autobiographical trilogy, Leduc movingly pleads her cause:

> They rejected the beginning of *Ravages*. It was a murder. They did not want the sincerity of Thérèse and Isabelle. They

were afraid of censure. Where is censure's true home? What are her habits, her manias? I can't work her out. I was building a school . . . a dormitory . . . a refectory . . . a music room . . . a courtyard . . . Each brick, an emotion. Each rafter, an upheaval. My trowel digging up memories. My mortar to seal in the sensations. My building was solid. My building is collapsing. Censure has pushed my house over with the tip of one finger. I had a pain in my chest the day I learned of their rejection. I was wounded right in my heart. Society opposes it even before my book can be published. My work is broken up, scattered. My searching through the darkness of memory for the magical eye of a breast, for the face, the flower, the meat of a woman's open sex . . . My searching, a box empty of bandages. Continue to write after such a rejection? I cannot. Stumps keep poking out of my skin.

De Beauvoir tried to offer *Ravages* to other publishers. In vain. They demanded more cuts. Leduc resigned herself to Gallimard's publication of her novel in a censored version in 1955. The book was praised by critics but had no commercial success. Then Jacques Guérin, a friend and patron of Leduc, brought out a private edition of *Thérèse et Isabelle* at his own expense, intended for a circle of fervent admirers of Leduc's work.

The censoring of *Ravages* and its lack of success contributed to Leduc's descent into paranoid delirium. She underwent electroshock therapy and took a long sleeping cure. But she lost neither her will to write nor her will to live.

At the beginning of the 1960s, on de Beauvoir's advice, Leduc grafted part of "Thérèse et Isabelle" into the third chapter of *La Bâtarde*. She took out passages, tightened up some pages, toned down some of the metaphors, modified the direction of certain dialogues. Thérèse metamorphosed into Violette. The rest of "Thérèse et Isabelle" was then published thanks to *La Bâtarde*'s success.

In 1966, taking heart from her new notoriety and doubtless out of a wish for "revenge," Leduc signed a contract with Jean-Jacques Pauvert. She had told Gaston Gallimard about this: "You will no doubt recall having rejected the first 500 pages of *Ravages*. This text later appeared in a limited edition. It was entitled *Thérèse et Isabelle*. Quite naturally, I am anxious to inform you that this same text is now scheduled to appear in a standard edition."

The publisher's call to order came straight away: "It was due to general agreement that we judged it preferable to postpone the publication of this text, which was at first destined to be part of *Ravages*. At the time, legal challenge was to be feared, which would have paralyzed this book's distribution among the bookshops, and so I left you free to publish *Thérèse et Isabelle* separately, in a private and limited edition, on the understanding that I would retain priority for a broader publication once circumstances allowed. But it was never a question of my rejecting this text."

Leduc bowed to the publisher's injunction, although, one must admit that he demonstrated a certain amount of dishonesty that day. *Thérèse et Isabelle* was swiftly printed by Gallimard and appeared in the bookshops in July 1966.

During the 1950s, unlike Jean Genet, Leduc had not benefited from a "louche" reputation nor from any public support as a famous writer. She had to wait until 1964 for that, when de Beauvoir wrote her preface to *La Bâtarde*.

It is the privilege of great artists to be ahead of their times. It is the lot of "accursed" ones to expect posthumous recognition. This is all the more true for women. Virginia Woolf foresaw Leduc's position, asserting that if a woman were to write accurately and precisely about her feelings, she would find no man—that is, no one at all—to publish her.

Now we have *Thérèse et Isabelle* as a whole work of art, with its original coherence and trajectory at last complete.

CARLO JANSITI

AFTERWORD

The list of early admirers of Violette Leduc is
literarily impressive: de Beauvoir, Cocteau,
Sartre, Genet, Camus, and Jouhandeau. In
a letter Simone de Beauvoir wrote to her
American lover, Nelson Algren, on June 28,
1947, de Beauvoir recounts having dinner
with Violette Leduc, whom she describes
as "the most interesting woman I know"
(Beauvoir 1998, 37). High praise indeed,
from someone like de Beauvoir. She is perhaps fascinated that someone from such
an underprivileged background, someone
with the odd and difficult personality that
was Leduc's, could produce such astonish-
ing writing, breaking new ground in the

description of women's lives and of female sexuality in particular.

Jean Cocteau wrote in a letter to an acquaintance in October, 1948: "Violette Leduc is a wonder and everything that comes out of her should find its way into the hands of anyone who knows how to read with their heart. *L'Affamée* needs no defense but times are hard. We have to help it along however we can" (Leduc 2007, 78n).

Yet for Leduc, being recognized by this elite subset didn't constitute a fully satisfying form of success—in part because she was poor and desperate to earn money from her writing, in part because she hungered for wider recognition.

Her first book, *L'Asphyxie*, translated as *In the Prison of Her Skin*, appeared in 1946, but it was only with the publication of *La Bâtarde* in 1964 when she was fifty-seven years old, that she found a larger reading public (at least in France), and with it a measure of financial stability. Until this success, she endured, as best she could, what was for her the extremely painful task of finding contentment in the admiration of a small number of readers.

To say that her early books sold poorly would be an understatement. There is a passage in her posthumously published volume, *La Chasse à l'amour* ("The Hunt for Love"), in which Leduc recounts the moment when she received a letter from her publisher, Gallimard, informing her that the remaining unsold copies of *L'Asphyxie* were about to be pulped:

> A letter from my publisher. Could it be good news? "My publisher." Who are you kidding. He's Proust's publisher. There's a clear difference between a cathedral of hawthorns and a louse coated with excrement. Let's open the envelope. My God! . . . They are going to pulp the remaining copies of *L'Asphyxie*. My book is dying. It never even really had a life. No one read it. Today is a day of mourning. I have lost a child . . .

The editor has run out of storage space. Did it really take up so much room in his cellars, my scrawny little kid? (Leduc 1994, 142–43)

A bit later on in the same passage from *La Chasse à l'amour*, Leduc realizes that Gallimard is actually offering her the chance to buy the remaining copies of *L'Asphyxie* at a reduced rate, and she imagines what she might do if she were able to afford to purchase all the copies Gallimard was about to destroy:

I read the letter again. I hadn't understood it fully. I have the chance to buy all the unsold copies before they are disposed of. There are 1,727 copies left. What will I do with them? Religious tracts. I'll ring doorbells and hand them out. They'll turn their dogs on me. Who believes in generosity any more? I'll sneak them into the bins of the booksellers that line the banks of the Seine before they even notice I've done it. I will go to the bookstore La Hune and,

fraudulently, I will place a single copy
on their shelves for the letter L. I will
sing "Death, where is your sting?" as I
leave La Hune. (143–44)

Leduc imagines buying her own books
from her publisher and then sneaking them
into places where, if someone should buy
them, the profits (at least the financial ones)
would not be hers. If she calls this a form of
fraud it is hardly because she is swindling
anyone financially, but rather because she
apparently feels her books would not have
legitimately earned the right to be on the
bookstore shelves where she herself would
have placed them.

Gallimard would once again return
L'Asphyxie to print after Leduc's 1964 success with *La Bâtarde*. It remains in print
today. Leduc would also receive a similar
letter from Gallimard regarding the fate of
the 1,473 remaining copies of her second
book, *L'Affamée*. At the bottom of the letter
she wrote, in response, "Pulp them! Pulp

them!" Her biographer, Carlos Jansiti, displays and reads from this letter in the recent documentary about Leduc, *Violette Leduc: La Chasse à l'amour*.

Leduc has become known as the author of books, fictional and autobiographical to varying degrees, (*Ravages, Thérèse and Isabelle, La Bâtarde*) which include scenes recounting sexual relations between women in vivid detail. Her books also include accounts of her unrequited love for a series of gay men (including Maurice Sachs, Jean Genet, and Jacques Guérin); her physical and emotional feelings for Simone de Beauvoir (never reciprocated across the several decades of their friendship—a word that perhaps cannot quite do justice to the odd and unbalanced relation they had); as well as her marriage and divorce, and her subsequent friendships and romantic relationships with a number of men. Illegitimacy

(Leduc's mother became pregnant with her by the son of a family for whom she was working) is at the heart of Leduc's personal and professional self-image. When she was in literary company, she often had difficulty fully accepting that she belonged where she was. In her writing, this self-doubt comes to be intimately tied to her sense of the unruliness of her own sexuality—an unruly sexuality that often provides the material about which she writes. Fascinated by sexual outsiders of many kinds, it does not seem that the categories that other people used to talk about her sexuality, or about sexuality in general, had much pertinence for her.

Consider the extraordinary letter she writes to de Beauvoir in late summer of 1950 about her feelings both for de Beauvoir and for a couple of women who run the hotel in which she is staying in the village of Montjean:

That you should not love in the way that I love you is well and good, since that way I will never grow tired of adoring you gravely. My love for you is a kind of fabulous virginity. And yet I have passed through, and am still in the midst of, a period of sexual frenzy. . . . I have been obsessed by, hounded by, that couple of women I wrote you about. I have been humiliated, revolted. They have found in this village, they have made real a union, whereas I have for 15 years been consumed by, and am still consumed by solitude. I have often felt as if I were in Charlus's skin as I spied on them, as I envied them, as I imagined them. They never even spend 15 minutes apart, and I often cry with rage and jealousy when I notice this fact. They are mistrustful, they are shut up inside their happiness. One night I told them, after all the people summering here had left, I told them in very nuanced terms that I loved you and about your beautiful friendship for me. It was a one-sided conversation. I gave, but got nothing in return. They are even more extraordinary than Genet's "Maids." The difference in their ages—I have also already told you about this, one is thirty, the other fifty-six—is something I find enchanting and consoling . . . How simple they are, I keep coming back to this, how unrefined, how sure of themselves. The younger one has the face of a brute. Their fatness is the weight of sensuality. When seated they open their legs wide, like soldiers, whereas so-called normal women keep them crossed or closed tight. They are a torment to me without even knowing it but they also intensify my love for you because you are a part of the disaster that I am. I often think about lesbians in their cabarets, who exist on another planet, who are nothing but sad puppets. (Leduc 2007, 174–75)

The letter is typical of Leduc in all her idiosyncrasy: verging here and there toward the preposterous without ever quite tipping over into it, excessive in its emotivity, self-consciously obsessive, and profoundly curious both about the way sexuality functions (which doesn't mean she can't make the odd homophobic remark), and about the lack of fit between her sexuality and everyone else's (in this case, de Beauvoir's, the two women she describes, and lesbians who frequent queer bars and cabarets). She is attentive to a number of characteristics, axes of variations in sexualities we might say, that aren't always factored into typical discussions of sexuality: that sexualities have a class or regional component; that age difference is important in some sexualities; that girth can have a relation to gender and to sexuality; that sexualities such as her own and that of this couple of women are often best understood by way of representations from the world of literature (Genet's two maids), and that the representations chosen can sometimes rely on transgendered forms of identification (her link to Proust's character, Charlus).

Consider another more condensed example of Leduc's attentiveness to the multivariable experience of sexuality. *La Bâtarde* recounts several outings taken by the young Leduc and her mother to see different shows while they were living under the same roof in Paris. (They once went, for instance, to see the cross-dressing aerialist, Barbette.) As they set out on one such outing, Violette takes her mother's arm:

> "Don't put your arm through mine. You're such a farm boy [*paysan*]!" she said.
> Farm boy. The use of the masculine really got to me. (2003, 127)

In one very compact utterance, Leduc's mother registers her impression of her daughter's sexuality, subtly linking together gender, object choice, and that odd mixture of regional identity, class, and race that is contained in the French concept of peasant, *paysan*. Leduc's representations of her mother's reactions to the sexually dissident forms of behavior she exhibits while growing up provide interesting evidence of a point of view (her mother's) that is neither exactly approving nor exactly disapproving, but is certainly matter of fact about such expressions of dissidence. When Leduc is expelled from her girls school because of her sexual relations with one of the teaching staff, she is sent by train to Paris, where her mother is now living. Her mother meets her at the station:

> I saw my mother in the first row: a brush stroke of elegance. A young girl and a young woman. Her grace, our pact, my pardon. I kissed her and she replied: 'Do you like my dress?' We talked about her clothes in the taxi. My mother's metamorphosis into a Parisienne eclipsed the headmistress and sent the school spinning into limbo. Not the slightest innuendo. Giving me Paris, she gave me her tact. (111)

There is a complicity between mother and daughter, a shared choice not to take up the subject of Leduc's behavior or its consequences. We might see behind this complicity a shared set of reference points regarding sexual culture. The sexual culture of the countryside, villages, and towns they came from was, while not the same as what they see around them in Paris, already a rich, diverse, and conflicted one, which means that they were both in full possession of a practical understanding of sexual diversity and dissidence that allowed them to communicate with and understand each other on all sorts of implicit levels.

This practical understanding of sexual diversity that Leduc shares with her mother is, of course, present in her letter to de Beauvoir as well. Her practical understanding tells her that her love for de Beauvoir, the relationship between the two women she encounters that summer, and the sexuality of Parisian lesbians are all related and yet different. We could say, borrowing the term mobilized so influentially by Kimberlé Crenshaw, that Leduc and her mother have a practical understanding of sexuality that is fundamentally *intersectional*. José Esteban Muñoz glossed Crenshaw's term in the following way: "Intersectionality insists on critical hermeneutics that register the copresence of sexuality, race, class, gender, and other identity differentials as particular components that exist simultaneously with one another" (Muñoz 1999, 99). We might well imagine that Leduc's experience of her own sexual idiosyncrasy, and her practical ways of understanding distinctions between different sexualities she perceives around her somehow involve an experience of intersectionality, and that among the identity differentials that count for her are differentials between country life, small town life, and city life, and also, the topic to which I now turn, differentials between people involved in literary or intellectual pursuits (herself, de Beauvoir) and those who are not.

However seriously Leduc may be taken by writers like Sartre, Jouhandeau, Cocteau,

Genet, and de Beauvoir, something about her being a woman means that both the social world and the gatekeepers of the literary field treat her differently than they treat, say, Genet. Leduc registers this aspect of her situation in many ways, including the portrayal, in *La Chasse à l'amour,* of the mental and physical distress she experiences following Gallimard's refusal in 1954 to publish those sections of her novel *Ravages* having to do with the sexual relations of Thérèse and Isabelle at boarding school (the text reprinted in this volume), the representation of an abortion and its aftermath, and several other passages. If these passages were so important to her, it is because she understood them to be a key part of her attempt to break new ground in literature, just as Genet was doing. One can also trace in her correspondence with de Beauvoir from a few years before this episode, her sense that de Beauvoir's *The Second Sex* had a similar kind of importance for the evolution of culture. She expresses her support for de Beauvoir as she confronted the violently misogynist reactions to her book, and she told her of her pride at being cited by de Beauvoir in the volume. "I thank you with all my heart for citing me on several occasions," she writes in 1949. "What touched me was the actual moment during which you were writing my name in a serious book" (Leduc 2007, 130).

Leduc's sense that she, Genet, de Beauvoir, and Sartre were breaking important new ground in the ways they struggled to represent sexualities that previously had no place in serious writing finds further expression in a letter from the following year. Early in 1950, Leduc makes a comparison between the audacity of Genet in his novels and the audacity of de Beauvoir in *The Second Sex:* "Genet's authority appears as strong as ever when you reread him. How salubrious are all the sexual audacities to be found in contemporary literature! I could feel the world-wide barrier of resistances begin to give way as I read volume 2 of *The Second Sex,* as I reread Genet" (Leduc 2007, 142). Clearly she meant for her own writing in these years to contribute to this same project. This helps explain why the frustrations of seeing her work censored, along with the frustration of the poor sales of her books, was almost too much for her to bear.

A scene in the recent French biopic devoted to Leduc develops this commonality, by showing de Beauvoir defending Leduc against her censors at Gallimard, accusing them of being unable to bear the idea of a woman speaking openly about sex between women, and insisting on the urgency for abortions—at the time illegal in France—to be a topic that could be written about in both literary and philosophical contexts (*Violette* 2014).

For Leduc, being involved with literature was part of her experience of sexuality.

Early in *La Bâtarde,* she describes for her readers how, around the age of sixteen, she related to a provincial bookstore:

> I also walked in the Place d'Armes on Saturday nights. The lighted storefronts crackled before my eyes. I was attracted, intrigued, spellbound by the yellow covers of the books published by the Mercure de France, by the white covers of the Gallimard books. I selected a title, but I didn't really believe I was intelligent enough to go into the largest bookstore in town. I had some pocket money with me (money that my mother slipped me without my stepfather's knowing), I went in. There were teachers, priests, and older students glancing through the uncut volumes. I had so often watched the old lady who served in the shop as she packed up pious objects, as she reached into the window for the things that people pointed out to her. . . . She took out Jules Romains' *Mort de quelqu'un* and looked at me askance. I was too young to be reading modern literature. I read *Mort de quelqu'un* and smoked a cigarette as I did so in order to savor my complicity with a modern

author all the more. . . . The Saturday after that I stole a book which I didn't read; but I paid cash for André Gide's *Les Nourritures terrestres* (*The Fruits of the Earth*) and a sculpture of a dead bird. Later, under my bedclothes, when I went back to boarding school, I returned to the barns, to the fruits of André Gide by the glow of a flashlight. As I held my shoe in the shoe shop and spread polish on it, I muttered: "Shoe, I will teach you to feel fervor." There was no other confidant worthy of my long book-filled nights, my literary ecstasies. (2003, 51–52)

Perhaps we could say that she experiences herself more as a member of a counterpublic than as a member of a public for the literature she explores. She is unable to relate to it in mainstream ways. She is too poor, too uncultivated, too young, too enthusiastic a reader to approach literature appropriately. Her reading is intermingled with other sensual experiences (cigarettes and the smell of shoe polish among them) in a way that enhances her sense of its illicitness. She, like many other alienated young people, often people exploring nonnormative sexual experiences, develops an affiliation with Gide's *The Fruits of the Earth*, a kind of countercultural classic of the early to mid twentieth century, with its call to a certain kind of sexual dissidence, to an experience of fervent sensuality.

Once she becomes a published writer, Leduc's relationship to bookstores takes on a different, more anxious cast. Here is a scene described in *Mad in Pursuit* that took place shortly after the publication of *L'Asphyxie* in 1946, a book that received only meager and unkind critical notices despite an excerpt having been published in Sartre's celebrated journal, *Les Temps Modernes*, and despite having appeared in a collection edited by Albert Camus:

> One afternoon I was preparing an assortment of vegetables to make my soup, a wild hope seized me, the knife fell onto my one sad leek. I threw on

my clothes. The journey to rue de Bac station was interminable. I arrived in front of the Gallimard bookstore on the Boulevard Raspail, in front of its eclectic windows, completely out of breath. But it must be in them. It wasn't. The large-format books, the rare editions of Valéry, of Gide, of Apollinaire, disdainful and withdrawn, rejected me utterly. The bastions of modern literature cannot be overthrown just to make way for your little pile of turds. Oh God, how I begged outside those windows . . . If I had only been sure of what I was writing, I should have been saved . . . Baudelaire and Rimbaud, were they sure of themselves? But I wasn't Baudelaire, I wasn't Rimbaud. Ten new books published every day. How can you expect them to display such a flood? An hour, even if it were just for an hour, each of us in turn . . . Where has it gone since I dedicated all those copies? Where has it gone to earth? Have the bookstores received it? I should die of shame if I had to ask them. Writing must be a sin, or why should I prefer to conceal it? My guilt was coming back. Window displays and bookstores whispered to me in the night: "You'll never amount to anything, you'll never amount to anything at all," just as my mother had once dinned those words into me in the past. I shall hand in my cards. Hand in your cards to whom? To the bookstores, to their windows, to the publisher. (1999, 72)

Perhaps foolishly, Leduc grants the window of the bookstore run by the publishing house Gallimard a particular kind of sacredness. Given how many famous authors Gallimard published, it was probably unreasonable to expect to find her own first book on display. And yet how is a new, idiosyncratic author of Leduc's ilk ever to find readers? Idiosyncratic books by idiosyncratic authors often circulate by word of mouth, developing small communities of highly partisan readers. Leduc already knew that this was the case for her first book, as she reveals a bit earlier in the same passage from *Mad in Pursuit*:

My cheeks still wet with tears, I ran into the antique dealer Hagnauer, who was only too delighted to give me the news that Cocteau had read my book and was telling everyone else to read it. Encouraged, I walked round for hours and hours. I had developed a method: that of the bird's nester. I slowed down when I was twenty yards away from the bookstore, then I stole up on it very gently so as to surprise my book in the window and receive a shock from it. But all the nests were empty. Except once. Where? The dispiriting window of the Polish bookstore on the Boulevard Saint-Germain. How old and worn it looked in the very back row! If I buy it from them, then they'll take it out of the window; if I buy it from them, it will become a dusty rectangle after I leave. I looked at it for a long time. (71–72)

Cocteau helped her book find readers in informal ways; its formal place in bookstores remained highly tenuous. Leduc knew that at the time Jean Genet's books circulated in a similar way: Genet's *Mira-cle of the Rose* was recommended to her by Simone de Beauvoir, but was not a text that was easy to find. It only existed in a hand-printed, 475-copy edition published by a small publishing house called Arbelète. De Beauvoir promised Leduc she would leave her copy of the novel for Leduc with the cashier at the Café des Deux Magots:

> The lady at the desk of the Deux-Magots handed me the copy of *Miracle de la Rose* Simone de Beauvoir had left there for me. It's heavy, I commented. Yes, it's heavy, the lady at the desk replied. . . . That evening *Miracle de la Rose* weighs down my bed. The book is inside a chest, between two covers that fit together. I have brought a deluxe edition home with me: it's a first. . . . The size and weight are almost those of a Bible at the foot of a pulpit. They require a lectern, special arrangements. I lean my elbow on the pillow, we tilt, the book and I together, towards the wall, and we begin to give ourselves to one

another. I am falling into my reading of *Miracle de la Rose* as one falls in love. (74)

Genet's book comes to Leduc through unofficial channels, we might say, and her reading of it resembles her youthful reading of Gide's *The Fruits of the Earth,* involving a combination of secrecy, sensuality, and sacredness. There is a lesson to be learned about the combination of these two phenomena, unofficial modes of circulation and a certain kind of fervent reading: they link both Genet and Leduc to what we might call a sexual counterpublic, a very specific kind of readership with a correspondingly particular kind of authorship and a particular experience of reading. Perhaps prominent display windows of imposing bookstores are not the most hospitable homes for books seeking that kind of readership, or offering that kind of experience.

Leduc's early work, with all the difficulties of its style, its subject matter, and its way of perceiving and thinking about the world, comes to be admired by much the same set of people who admired Genet's early work. The book-collecting industrialist Jacques Guérin would even arrange for the publication of a private, luxury collector's edition of *L'Affamée*, similar to the private editions of Genet's early novels. It was, in fact, in the form of this private edition that Leduc's book would find itself where she had dreamed it would be. As her biographer Carlo Jansiti notes, the private edition "comes off the presses in September 1948. Paul Morihien, rue de Beaujolais, dedicates a window to it" (Jansiti 1999, 210); Morihien was also the publisher of the private edition of Genet's *Our Lady of the Flowers*. The more affordable Gallimard edition of *L'Affamée*, published a few months later, sold poorly.

Unlike Genet, Leduc was slow to find

a wider readership. De Beauvoir's understanding of why Leduc's *Ravages* was censored more rigorously than anything by Genet ever was is simple and convincing: the men who chose what to publish, the men who reviewed what was published, the men who demanded that this or that passage be censored were made uncomfortable by the idea and by the example of a woman finding a vibrant new language in which to explore instances of female same-sex sexuality (the topic of *Thérèse and Isabelle*), or to recount the experience of a botched abortion, or to describe bemusedly what it is like to handle a penis during a taxi ride. Yet, there is perhaps more to be understood about the difficulty Leduc has had finding readers, the slowness with which they have found their way to her writing. Perhaps there is a kind of complexity to the reading experience she offers that has been difficult to take in, perhaps there is a complexity to her exploration of the way sexual experience is constructed, and to the way sexual and literary experiences intermingle that have been difficult to access. What to do? Find more of her books and make special arrangements to read them: polish your shoes, hide under the sheets with her books, display her books wherever likely readers might find them. Speak to others fervently about your obsession, about the unsettling complexity of the sexual and literary experiences that Violette Leduc offers.

MICHAEL LUCEY

WORKS CITED

Beauvoir, Simone de. 1998. *A Transatlantic Love Affair: Letters to Nelson Algren.* New York: The New Press.
Jansiti, Carlo. 1999. *Violette Leduc.* Paris: Grasset.

Leduc, Violette. 1994. *La Chasse à l'amour.*
Paris: Gallimard-Imaginaire. [Original
edition 1972].

———. 1999. *Mad in Pursuit,* trans. Derek Coltman. New York: Riverhead Books.
[Original edition 1970].

———. 2003. *La Bâtarde,* trans. Derek Coltman.
[Normal, IL]: Dalkey Archive Press.
[Original edition 1964].

———. 2007. *Correspondance 1945–1972,* ed. Carlos Jansiti. Paris: Gallimard, 2007.

Muñoz, José Esteban. 1999. *Disidentifications:
Queers of Color and the Performance of
Politics.* Minneapolis: University of Min-
nesota Press, 1999.

Violette. 2014. Directed by Martin Provost.
Diaphana. DVD.

Violette Leduc: La Chasse à l'amour. 2013.
Directed by Esther Hoffenberg. Les
films du poisson. DVD.

TRANSLATOR'S ACKNOWLEDGMENTS

Thanks to Deborah Levy, Zoe Crisp, Sophie and Jean-Dominique Langlais, Clémence Sebag, Cécile Menon, and Hilary Kaplan; your contribution to this translation was essential.

SOPHIE LEWIS, 2011

The Feminist Press is a nonprofit educational organization founded to amplify feminist voices. FP publishes classic and new writing from around the world, creates cutting-edge programs, and elevates silenced and marginalized voices in order to support personal transformation and social justice for all people.

See our complete list of books at
feministpress.org

THE FEMINIST PRESS
AT THE CITY UNIVERSITY OF NEW YORK
FEMINISTPRESS.ORG